First published in 2010
By
Maley World Marketing

Cover photograph: Chem trails over Saddleworth – James Loughlin
                  Chem trail photo on page 155 – James Loughlin

To all those beautiful misfits who have bravely stepped out of what a manipulated society classes as the norm. Those who refused to be seduced into docile acquiescence, and who have found their truth, spoke their truth, and been ridiculed by the very people they tried to inform and protect.

We can stop them

They will come you know, if we don't stop them
Right now they are polishing their fascist boots and loading their taser
guns with electricity
A single brain washed cell receiving shouted orders from delusional
Police sergeants and demonic sergeant majors who think they know the
plan
But that plan will eventually take their children too, as well the non-
conformist's children
They'll be no reward for the uninformed uniformed
No loaded onto trucks though, like in the decaying footage of a world
war two film
Much craftier than that
You will be taken with full blessing of the EU, UN, NAFTA and NATO
Placed in the concentration camps which are already waiting, cold and
menacing, for the people daring to question government policy, which
now apparently, makes you a terrorist
War on terror is war on freedom
When you look closely it all works in reverse
Whatever is said the opposite is meant
And freedom has become a curse

Soon we will hear the marching of the robots
Not just in Iran, Iraq, Afghanistan and Haiti
But in your village and mine
They have collected all your data on the internet and labelled you
dangerous because you bought homeopathic medicine two years ago
How dare you choose what's right for your body
Refuse the microchip?
Deny our vaccines?
This is how easily you will be took
They will sit and study your facebook account with its connection to the
C.I.A.
Have your laugh then take a look
This is fascism the modern way

The craft manipulators and naïve enforcers are false friends in this master plan
User and used they will march gallantly into your family home and remove you and your beliefs; you and your terrorist aroma therapist lifestyle
You and your bag of aborted dreams
And this is not an apocalyptic apology from a despondent doomsday theorist
I have merely opened my eyes and seen what is here now
Not what is coming in some far off period of time so it won't affect you
What is already in place as we sit watching the X factor and the ironically named Big Brother

But listen
Today it is not too late
The end is not written yet
Something can be still be done
And it can all be done by you, in one day
Switch off the T.V. and see how mesmerised we have become
Switch on to the powerful, multi dimensional being you are capable of becoming
Let them know we know where the power lies
Drip by drip till it tips
No more talk of cultural, religious, political differences
Let's talk about the things that connect us
The beautiful children we have, the wonder of nature, oceans and sunsets, animals and mountains, we share them all don't we?
Show them that we love each other and we will not be divided
And that we know what their game is and that we refuse to play anymore
Stand united, arm in arm, without any labels or barriers
Loosen the gruesome grip of identity
Be peaceful in protest, never violent
Tell them they are forgiven and they can leave quietly
Love, peace, freedom and paradise are only one thought away
Get thinking

Author's note

"We are waking up" is a fictitious novel and the author holds no responsibility for anyone who extracts information and applies it in any way. The author does not give medical advice or prescribe the use of any technique as a form of treatment for physical or medical problems without the advice of a doctor. In the event you use any of the information in this book for yourself the author and publisher assume no responsibility for your actions. If there is any information in the book which is of interest to you I whole heartedly encourage you to go and research it and draw your own conclusions.

The photographs are a combination of my own and those of Wasyl Kolesnikov 7th dan international Aikido instructor, who kindly allowed me to use examples of his work. His contact information can be found at the back of the book.

1

BEGINNINGS

In truth there is no beginning and no end. We have eternity woven into the fabric of our existence.

"Definitely green," Joseph said, surveying the icicle shapes that hung down from illusory ceilings of twisted rock.

"Aw we'll never agree on colour, you can't keep your mind on one shade for a start, changing it with every thought, it's impossible," Annie replied, manifesting an index finger to wag with.

"Alright, but you can't deny the fact they are reaching down in endless anticipation of the day they make contact with their opposite floor based stalagmites, well you can't can you?"

"No, I'll give you that one, a dramatic, stalagmatic love story for certain."

They were right on the romance bit, in truth, as it was indeed nicely enhanced, courtesy perhaps of the golden rays which shone down from invisible floodlights, a mystical hue deftly created on the surface of a lazy lake.

Then there were the small drifting boats, decked out with luminescent lights, carrying musicians playing exquisite songs, steeped in overtones and sonic formulas, merely for their own pleasure of course, any external appreciation being nothing more than accidental bonus.

The lake itself was perfectly still; reflecting everything clearly, like a mind without worries. Well, that's why they always go there to make their big decisions, those old friends, (mine too actually, but more of that in a moment) resting and re energising for long periods of our manufactured time, unshackled and weightless, febrile feathers refusing all anchors.

The goodbyes would be temporary; they knew this for certain, and arrangements for re unions where word was the bond were being candidly made.

We return there many times, to that between-worlds realm, returning to tell stories of our lives on Earth in our skin and bone suits. I say we, because normally, and only normal for us here of course, but a surreal state of affairs in your shoes, yes normally, I, Conrad the story teller, would have been a part of it all. Resigned however, but by no means relegated to the post of observer and universal journalist, I will endeavour to tell all. Story telling, that's my thing see, we all have work to do here and this is mine.

You know how hard it can be saying goodbye to friends don't you? Well it gets even trickier here. You won't remember, I know, but concepts and ideas are so finely tuned that journey and destination are achieved by mere thought, mere thought and that's it. And concentrating on a place or a thing, well that's enough to make it instantly manifest.

"Any pain there then?" I'm sure I heard you ask.

Bodily pain does not exist of course, took its redundancy package and left for Planet Earth long ago, and the soul, that cleverly concealed, ill thought of concept beneath the bones knows true peace and comfort.

Try to imagine a light so intense it draws the soul towards it, pulling it magnetically to its power source. Go on try. Did you do it? The love displayed here is real, magnanimous and unconditional, a state far beyond the limitations of uttered words. And a bit more than a wet lick in the ear too.

So from this Cosmic Pontins they will begin to plan out and literally choose (yes of course they choose) all the events and situations that will materialise in their future incarnations. They will be allowed opportunities to correct any wrong doings they have caused people in past lives and will choose with total honesty an existence to facilitate spiritual growth. (You can escape it though, all possibility is available.)

Joseph, the old soul had decided he was ready for another trip out; great deliberation had taken place about what he most needed to learn from his visit. That's the reason they were all at "Golden Cavern" awaiting the narrative of the next instalment in Joseph's journey.

There was music too, I told you that before, and the air was filled with the scent of pine needle, well apart from the scent Delmore breathed, he always preferred lavender you see, and breathing, if I can just clarify, optional not essential.

They arrived on the thought train, craftily carried on tracks of truth, Joseph, Kitty, Delmore, Jack, Annie, Florence and Robert, deeply connected through numerous adventures, losing and finding each other sort of adventures, happy and sad adventures, but always returning home to share their stories and experiences. Yes, storytellers if you like, in the vault of the afterlife.

With experience comes wisdom, not intelligence, that's not wisdom at all. They had enough to know now that the more things that happened to them on their travels, the more diverse roles they played out, the more knowledge and experience they would bring back home to share with each other.

"I'll assume you know why we are here today?" Joseph said, tilting his illusory head, the way he does with important announcements, always to the left.

"The pull of that wonderful planet is getting stronger moment by moment, forcing my hand if you like. I need another great earthly adventure, another lesson to progress, and I must tell you the thought of Planet Earth has seduced me into making a decision, a decision which will one way or another affect us all."

Fake surprise reigned momentarily but its cover was quickly blown by the reality of the truth that they all had secretly known what was coming.

"I have been resting and reflecting long enough my dears, another journey is necessary for my overall growth, back to that freewill fairground, up and down, round and round, loop the loop world," he declared, tracing loops through the air for emphasis and adding an orange glow to the foray, a sparkler against a blackened sky.

"Must conquer that earthly idiot in me this time too; work on my ability to give for the joy of giving with no thought of receiving in return of course, to master the arduous art of compassion. You know what a weakness this has been on my last few visits. To discover the reason why I seem to excel in selfish behaviour when I return to Earth will be enough of a mission. Maybe I pitch the circumstances too high, or maybe it's just the density of the planet. I do hope one more trip will be sufficient and I can move onto learning and mastering other areas of my character, so many dimensions to work up to you know." He elongated his size with the word dimensions before resuming his rhetoric.

"There is a family under the irrefutable spell of maternal longing; the niggling nudge of parenthood will soon be the full on shoulder charge that finally bowls them over. Future mother and father are quite poor too, and the mother is also in bad health, I have been with them many times already; looking good, I'm sure you agree, looking good. It's just a matter of waiting for the embryonic phase to complete and my consciousness will be visiting briefly. Two nights half board," he joked, puffing out two bright red cheeks with exaggerated laughter.

"The arrangements have been loosely made, it has been agreed, it's earthbound for me my friends. Do we have any takers on a joint trip; you know we can look for an opportunity to make it happen?"

Annie who had been hovering around the peripheries stopped quickly, attention sufficiently held. She was the closest to Joseph you see, no doubt there, but she was also the one whom he had most earthly conflict with, brothers who fought over anything and everything, with one of their worst arguments ending up in the accidental death of Annie. (I say accidental from the Earth perspective of course) Business partners in Greece who amassed a fortune as shipping magnates, but through the greed of Joseph (I know, there are two sides to one of your Earth coins) and the weakness of Annie to deal with him, (there you go, scales balanced) they lost everything, fortune, freight and friendship.

Another incarnation saw them as husband and wife in a dysfunctional, loveless marriage, a gamut of emotionally charged liaisons they proudly owned, avid collectors of requisite relationships.

Although at the time, undeniably terrible disasters they provided vital experience for their progress, and when each particular life came to an end they were able to calmly assess their mistakes and thank each other for playing their roles so well.

"I'll go for it," Annie shouted, both hands flat on her head, a highlighted posture to suit the monumental decision made.

"Yes, I'll risk the wrath of your earthly lunacy; it will be good to resolve our differences there, you know, a clean slate and all that."

Joseph nodded reflectively, as if in deep thought, but secretly he was delighted to have the opportunity for a positive experience with Annie on Earth. He felt as if all conflicts should be resolved this time.

"I too would like that," he eventually replied, inhaling on an imaginary cigar for his own amusement and Annie's too. Annie smiled at his idiosyncratic behaviour and the way he always sacrificed his credibility for the price of a cheap joke.

They amused each other for a while, pondering over the many different situations and roles they could opt for, entertaining each other with exaggerated predicament.

Being in spirit form of course, where time is not linear, they had the advantage of being able to see roughly how their life on planet Earth would pan out, not every detail, but a kind of overview.

They continued to stretch their imagination for a while longer, fantastically created incarnations abound, before Joseph finally turned serious and got down to business, calling for assistance from Dolan, spirit guide and overseer of his new incarnation.

Between the two of them they looked at the map of events and possible paths. It appeared as though Joseph, who would be in female form, would be offered a path where she could become pregnant around the eighteenth year of that life, and if she wanted it to be so at that time, and all went well, that is when Annie would join her.

She agreed she would wait for this occasion, knowing that eighteen linear Earth years are not like eighteen years in the spirit world. Not like it all.

And so it was agreed right there, right then, they would become mother and daughter in a brave attempt to work through their previous conflicts, also allowing Joseph the opportunity to strengthen his weaknesses and master the art of giving unconditionally.

Kitty, Delmore, and Robert's sense of adventure was also being stimulated; taking only a little more warm conversation before they too enthusiastically agreed to return.

Kitty, the one who had suffered tremendous restriction in her last two lives felt like she had experienced this aspect enough to move on and benefit from the challenge she had bravely accepted long ago. The thought of a life with more freedom and adventure was certainly a temptation to her. Mothering and nurturing; well she was an expert at them. She told the others she was going to sit by the tree at "Old Mellow meadow," the tree being the undisputed champion of energy and wisdom. Kitty knew it would inspire and give her the strength she needed for dealing with the challenge of change.

It greeted her with the warmth of an old friend, lifting her instantly, energy from one form to another. She admired its great beauty, motionless, and bathed in surreal sunlight. These same kind of special moments and opportunities are available every day on Earth of course, but not many people notice or appreciate them, too busy, too ignorant, and then too late.

She sat for what would have been hours in the land of the clock, soaking up the dynamic energy before returning to the others.

Delmore is an artist; he plays with colours, serious about it too, revered here in fact, but nursing a great earthly craving to reach his potential elsewhere.

Things have never really worked out for him see, well not in that way, and the fact he has never fulfilled himself creatively had left him more and more frustrated. It was a close thing in his last incarnation though, really close. He showed great potential as a painter but had agreed pre birth to be removed from the world before reaching adulthood, a train crash, naively labelled an accident, taking both his and his mother's life. He knew this time though he had to achieve creative closure, he felt it strongly, one more chance to sing, to dance, to write or paint, just some way of taking his cosmic talent across dimensions.

To do this, Delmore would need to be meticulous in choosing the incarnation to best facilitate it, and he would not be alone in the planning. Well, you never are are you.

A blast of excitement shot through him and left him wondering why he had waited so long to move on. Hastily the others were informed that he too was also ready to leave for the blue spinning ball and would be making preparations to look for an opening that would allow his dreams to unfold.

"Anyone else for the universal roller coaster? Hop on board, return tickets only."

Robert shuffled excitedly before steadying himself and leaping in the gap.

"I'm game, I've been thinking since Joseph broke his news, I can't be absolutely certain, things are so incredible here and it's become really hard to leave, but I think I am ready, yes I am ready, I think," he said, not convincing anyone.

"Such paradise, such paradise, it really is the hardest thing to go, but I know we must keep travelling and learning, it's our purpose. I really would like the opportunity to be with you Kitty, whenever you go I mean. I could try to help you find your joy and freedom; the same way you helped me last time when my mind was lost. Oh you do deserve it Kitty," he said, bouncing like a puppy on a trampoline and drawing her closer.

"I would love to go with you and try, would you allow me the great honour?"

"What do you think?" she said, her inflexion implying that the answer to the question was glaringly obvious.

"I am very grateful Kitty; we have a lot to look forward to."

She sent her gratitude silently. A great silence also filled the Cavern. Boats passed by once more and the quiet was broken by scintillating music, riding invisible thermals and surfing energy waves to envelope the listener. When they were ready to communicate again the music faded, maximising the potential for clarity of thought. Jack and Florence felt all eyes were on them.

Jack had suffered great tragedy on his last visit, both parents killed when he was only nine years old. He also lost a child of his own later in life, a great part of his life was spent in pain and suffering.

At the time he thought he would never feel happiness again, earthly emotions trapped under suffering skin. Yet as soon as that life was over he fell straight into the arms of his family who were routinely waiting for his arrival, pain and heartache instantly dissolved in the relief of the reunited.

The density and struggle of Jack's last life had assisted his overall growth and understanding tenfold. The heaviness of grief was soon forgotten as weightlessness cut through strings of fear and doubt and released him to the bliss he now basked in. His only regret was that he didn't enjoy more of his life whilst he lived on Earth, such a common regret. He knew he should have trusted more.

Joseph was always telling him he was too hard on himself.

"Remember Jack, it's easy to judge things from here when we can see all the reasons why things happen and are privileged with knowledge of the outcomes. When you are down there with only your five senses and a three dimensional field to play in, it is a much more difficult game. So it is important to try to keep connected with your higher self and trust in the bigger picture. Earth life has a habit of cutting you off from your supply. You should go easy on yourself."

Wisdom flowed from many lifetimes of experiences and Jack felt each statement hit him with the clarity of a well struck bell.

"I understand what you say Joseph, I am just so happy and content at the moment. I think I need to be with my loved ones for a while yet, we will move on together when the time is right, just not yet.

I'm not afraid," he added, instantly designing a warrior stance for any non believers of his statement.

"I am healed now, painless in fact; you don't know how good that feels Joseph, of course I am reluctant to risk it just yet."

"Well it is always about choice Jack, you choose the suffering and you choose the pleasure. Take all the time you need, you have a never ending supply of it," he joked, straightening the Sergeant major moustache he had chosen for the day.

He informed the others of his decision to stay home. They were happy for him of course, knowing with certainty they would see him on their return.

Florence had decided to stay too. She was very close to Jack and they had followed each other through numerous experiences.

"We will stay for a while and wait until you return," Jack repeated. "The perfect party planners for the home comers."

So on that day without a name, at a time that can't be measured, in a place that they created with their thoughts, agreements of cast iron were made.

"We will get together again and enjoy our last few times here before we prepare for our journey," Joseph said, head tilted once more and an air of superiority shown.

A split second later he was gone, smugly reappearing in the "The Garden of Thought." He needed time to relax and work on his energy. It was going to be a challenging time ahead and he needed to focus himself, plug any leaks and refill on the purist of energy.

He thought about the words he would use to motivate his friends in preparation for their trip. This he always did just before a big event and there was no bigger event than leaving this lightness and brightness, especially for the density of Earth.

A human being is seen as the highest Earth form you can take, yet is nearly always the most challenging and complex of existences. The human is also seen as the most evolved and intelligent species, yet when you look at the state of the world there is little evidence of this actually being true.

As well as numerous human incarnations, Joseph held vague memories of being birds and other animals, and remembered it being a much more simplistic and free existence. He even had the feeling there had been incarnations when he was no more than the sound of a falling rock, or a momentary flash of lightning, all steps to becoming the wizened soul he now is, tiny pieces of a jigsaw with no ending.

I, Conrad, previously introduced as cosmic tale teller, have no recollection of any life besides a human one. Joseph however feels what he feels, and he has validity in those feelings. So let's go back to his garden and the utter contentment he felt there, it's not his fault after all, the misjudgement, the speed of re entry, I mean he had no idea how quick things were about to change did he?

2

MOVING ON

There is no material thing in the whole of the universe that you can hold on to forever. The people you bond with in love however will be impossible to shake off.

Firstly there were the flashes of light; bright and pulsating, followed by the gentle beginnings of the powerful, magnetic pull.

His energy began changing rapidly and he knew for sure that on Earth his new human form was ready to be inhabited. It took him by surprise however; it was sooner than he had anticipated.

He shouted to his friends, at least he must be allowed to say goodbye he thought, even if there was no time for anything else. His anxious thoughts were received by us all I must add, and I, the assigned reporter of the events which are taking place, had to remain impartial.

He tried to focus on his friends to draw them in, but he was being pulled ever quicker to Earth, a vortex of colours, swirling and pulsating, drawing him deep down into their centre.

Annie, dithering as she was in the distance, relocated herself, quick as an alpine pig, but not quick enough. Joseph tried to communicate something to her but it was all too late. She stood there in disbelief, cursing her own poor timing.

The sadness she felt was mirrored by the changing scenery; the beauty of the place disappearing down black holes of negativity, colours paled and a cold black mist rolled in. Forecast, impending storm.

She took stock, did Annie, quickly reminding herself there was nothing to fear, Joseph was infinite energy and could never die, he was merely on his way to another experience, to a world of illusion that everyone thinks is real.

One by one the rest of them arrived.

"It's too late," Annie cried. "Joseph has gone."

No more words were spoken. Their wisdom was such that they knew questions were of no use now. They would move forward and use it to create a positive outcome and they knew exactly how and what to think about.

The pasture is shocking, visually speaking, in its vibrancy, intensity and vividness. You'd say so too, those flowers, such intricate and complex designs, natural patterns and colour arrangements impossible to emulate synthetically. You've got them too, I know, but generally, and understandably of course, what with your televisions, laptops, facebooks, ipads, iphones, ipods, e mails and ear phones, the focus of attention necessary to see real beauty is, as I said, generally absent.

Still, the old flower doesn't care if anyone sees it or not, it will always unfold to its maximum potential and beauty, in the same way the birds do, singing their little dawn chorus, regardless of who listens.

"Well everybody, Joseph is on his journey now, soon to be born once more, head first into the unknown with all the courage of a lion," Jack said, wondering momentarily how well he would be able to step into Joseph's cosmic footsteps.

"Let's take a moment to send him our thoughts and wish him good things, what do you say?"

They stood quietly, shook out any negativity and extended their positivism, enhanced by heartfelt belief, outwards towards Joseph.

The shock of his sudden departure soon diminished, talking as they did, about this and that, talking amongst the incredible beauty of the flowers. Well it lifted their spirits a great deal, that free gift for the aware and appreciative did.

"If I could take just one observation to the world, it would be that everything we have here we also have there. It's only our ignorance and the way we are programmed that stops us living an incredible..."

"Quick, look," shouted Delmore, cutting dead Jack's observation, eye brows arched and dropped jaw selected, eyes full of imminent adventure. "Look in the centre of that flower. It's Joseph's face."

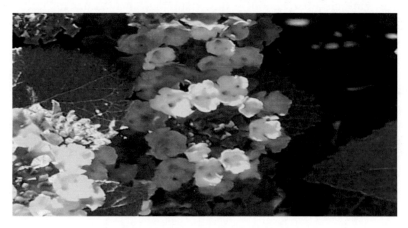

They walked over to where Delmore was standing and guess what; they did see the face of Joseph appearing in the pinkness of that flower. (Conrad airs caution here, but maybe not enough.)

I bet you'll struggle with that one, "how can that be possible?" you'll be saying to yourself. "Nonsense," you might shout, scrutinising those flowers with sceptical spectacles. But the thick moustache will appear, then the Roman nose and those deep-set all knowing eyes. You'll see.

"I knew it; I knew he wouldn't leave like that, not without a sign or something. We must never forget to look for signs, they are always around us. The universe is speaking all the time; we must learn its language."

The sigh from Annie was a deep, dramatic one, as she declared the sign from Joseph was a certain reminder that they would always be together, and also validation she suspected, that he had arrived safely.

Just for your jottings, distance is only ever the difference between two points. When the gap is filled with love, then the further apart the points the more love between them and the closer it can feel. Not convinced? I thought not.

She will enjoy her time here now; hanging out with her favourite people, knowing that quality is possible in all the moments that will build the bridge to her reunion with Joseph. She will also carry on sending him guidance and direction, knowing of course the moment he is born he will forget her and everything about his purpose and mission. This is law. She just hoped his path and the people he met on it would encourage and facilitate an environment where he was connected to the source, and maybe, a great big fat overly ambitious maybe, he would keep the contact open. Well, you have to hope don't you?

3

FOCUS

The mind leads every movement of the body. You cannot raise a finger without the mind initiating it. Learn to focus your mind or it will drag your body through disaster after disaster.

Meanwhile life went on for Annie and the gang, the way life goes on. Delmore kept himself busy creating stunning scenery and landscapes for the others to enjoy, a vigorous training programme for his up coming visit to Earth.

To be honest, I think he was secretly hoping he could carry some of his talent across with him by preloading his soul with all things creative, smuggling talent through the cosmos and arriving innocently at the birth canal, casually strolling through the "nothing to declare" gate.

He understood how to make use of his intent and to make it work for him. He knew that wherever you put your attention and focus, there would also be energy flowing there, a point sadly missed by most people on Earth. Calm down! Calm down! I missed it too.

So many afraid, so many fearful, yet constantly thinking about the thing that is making them fearful, trapping the energy and creating the reality of what they fear. Yet it is so simple to reverse.

Instead of focusing on weakness they simply have to focus on being strong. If they are worried about being ill, how about celebrating the health they do have every day. And if they are stuck in poverty, why not see themselves as having everything they need and to see the great abundance of nature. Hold on to the thought until it materialises; hold on no matter what. The law of attraction is a reality that can be proved through its application. The truth however, is, that it is difficult to begin this concept if we are in poverty, pain, or not knowing when we will eat next. But begin we must. No thought is irrelevant, they are all little magnets and you must decide whether yours are positively or negatively charged.

Whether you agree with this universal law or not, you are deeply engrossed in its mechanics, passive observation not being an option, thoughts and expectations magnetising situations which resonate on a similar frequency to the thinker and thought. It seems silly not to put your cosmic order form in and attract something worthwhile.

I know, I know, you have been thinking positively for six months, two weeks and three days and the cat just ate your vanilla slice. Well, let me give you a little tip from the realm of more than three dimensions. A thought obviously comes from the mind or the brain, but thinking alone will not do it, if you think it will, think about thinking again. You need to add another factor to ignite the thought form.

Alright I'm going to use scientific terms for the next few minutes, I know how much you earthlings love your scientific proof.

When the heart is measured with an electrocardiogram, its electric signal is somewhere near sixty times greater than the electric signal from the brain, measured on an EEG. Now then, the hearts magnetic field can measure up to five thousand times stronger than that of the brain, and both of those fields have the ability to change the energy of atoms. So the thought is one aspect of the dynamic, while the other one comes from the heart and is known as belief. And when you believe something in your heart, it creates an electrical and magnetic expression which can literally change the reality in which you are experiencing.

This electricity and magnetism oscillates as energy waves which interact with the world and universe, manipulating your life's events minute by minute. If this is too much to comprehend, think for a moment about the placebo effect you have very cleverly used in your medical field. Oh and your scientific research and collected data will validate all this, so relax, its all above board.

When a tablet made of sugar, nothing more, or some similar substance, is administered and is claimed as the new cure for cancer for example, the recipient, who believes the claim, can physically have tumours disappear from the body. Not just in one experiment, but thousands. This indicates to Uncle Conrad that a thought coupled with a belief in your heart can change the physicality of what you may call reality. On the other hand, if the doctor you believe so unquestioningly says you only have a few months to live, rest assured you will be gone before he receives his next bonus for vaccinating against the lying swine flu.

Let's take it one step further if you will allow. If we can heal our cells and change the physicality of them through thought coupled with heartfelt belief, can we not attract and dispel events and situations which also carry molecular structure?

I suggest to you, just my opinion, nothing to worry about, take it or leave it, but I suggest that more than attracting or repelling, we are literally writing the world as we go. That means in simpler terms, you can have health, abundance, peace and loving relationships as the world changes to suit your belief patterns. Be careful with it though, you have to know what you really believe, deep in the subconscious and not what you think you believe or would like to believe.

Another thing while I'm on a rant, there is absolutely no reason why your cells and organs have to give in after seventy or eighty years, no scientific findings whatsoever. So here is my last question for you, if you haven't scientifically fallen asleep yet. Is it possible that our deepest heartfelt beliefs tell us that seventy or eighty years is around the mark our bodies can survive to, and therefore our cells come to agree with this belief pattern, electrically communicated of course from the brain and the hearts magnetic field, (remember the scientific tests with your machines) and respond accordingly by shutting down? There you go. That's it, back to the law of attraction.

It is a disappointment to see this concept which has now been globally popularised sadly concentrated solely on material gain. Too much emphasis is currently on the individual creating material abundance for them and them alone. "Just focus on that lovely blue Mercedes and watch it fall from the sky." Now depending on the individual's ability to focus, it will certainly bring results, but in vastly varying time scales. The downside to this of course, is that the whole emphasis is on individual materialism. Now I think I know you well enough to say that you wouldn't really be happy with a brand new Mercedes while the family across the street cannot pay their grocery bill, and their ten year old child has never seen the seaside? Some will I guess, but the majority I feel not.

Abundance is a wonderful and natural state to be in, so if you achieve it, share it. Buy yourself a coach and a hotel and go pick up those children who have never been to the seaside, then you can enjoy watching them have fun and subtly teach them how they too can achieve abundance.

And if you are one of those people who know that this system of manipulating your reality through thought and intent works, you could use it to bring an end to poverty and suffering for all of humanity, collectively hold on to a thought form that sees the collapse of any system which allows such injustices to thrive. You could use this law of attraction to see the whole of humanity have an equal chance at some form of happiness, end all wars and bring peace to the planet. It would bring much more joy than the short lived satisfaction of owning a new piece of blue metal.

So off you go, gather your folks and get manipulating, you'll be amazed at the results and at just how few people you need doing it to impact reality.

My good friend Delmore, he knows how to apply these laws, a shrewd dude if I ever knew one, a determination like you would not believe. If he feels something inside of him, a desire to do something, a wish to see someone, a need to visit somewhere, he just does it. He never lets his mind (or anyone else's) talk him out of it. If you were here now he would tell you himself.

"Every time we follow our heart it is always 100% correct," he'd say. "Even when we follow our intuition and the outcome is completely different than we thought, it is the thought that is wrong not the intuition. The intuition took you to the situation for your growth. Growing is not always easy. Sometimes the things we want are not the things we need," he would probably add. That's how he is. You see he knows every thought is critical. He makes sure he is in charge of what goes in and out of his mind, cultivating powerful and loving thoughts to ensure he is master of his own destiny.

What about Florence and Jack? What were they up to? Oh yeah, I had to tell you they were content to bask in the blissfulness of projected thought form for the time being, and to add, that they would know when the time was right to expand their experience and add to the totality of what they were. They are experienced travellers and when change is necessary for them, they will recognise the powerful feeling.

A bulb cannot stay a bulb when its destiny is to be a flower. Eventually the compulsion to grow and to change overpowers the fear to stay as you are. Yes they would know alright, so don't worry about them.

Robert and Kitty would soon begin planning their next adventure too. Actually they will be the next ones to leave. Delmore will follow and then Annie will be joining Joseph. Changes are imminent, big or small will be a matter of perspective.

4

OPPORTUNITY

Trapped under clay and concrete the weed saw a tiny speck of sunlight. Grateful of the opportunity, it twisted, turned and grew towards the pinprick of light until eventually it squeezed through and out, displaying all its beauty in the glorious sunshine.

It was shortly after the departure of Joseph and the face in the flower day, when the attention of the gang was drawn to a new arrival.

Jack had tuned into the energy of a young spirit who had been taken from her world quickly and was in a deep state of shock. They all tried to reassure her with open hearts and the declaration that she would be alright, ignoring for the moment the great fear enveloping the girl.

It was a long time before she spoke, and for the last time, I use time as a framework for the earthling, I'll not be mentioning that again.

"Where am I?" she pleaded, scanning the unfamiliar with eyes of trauma and trepidation.

Jack was first to answer, faster than Kim Carsons if I remember.

"You are in a different dimension that's all, please try not to worry, you are very safe," he said quietly, hoping whispering would help.

"In the words of your world, you have died. Of course you are still very much alive, that's why we never use the word died. We prefer the word changed."

"But I can still see my body beneath me, and who are those people around me?"

"They must be trying to bring you back," Annie added.

"I don't want to go back, my body hurts down there. There was an accident, I remember, a car, darkness. Oh look who's there, my mum is standing beside me. I can see her now. Am I supposed to go back?"

"I am not sure," said Jack, genuinely not sure. "Do you want to?"

The girl looked around in desperation; trying to establish a fraction of familiarity to assess her new surroundings with, conscious of the fact a monumental decision had to quickly be made.

"It's so incredible here; I've never felt peace like it. I don't know if I can go back," she added, already succumbing to the pulsating paradise. "Look at the colour of those flowers. I've never seen anything like that, and that lake, is it real?"

Jack lifted a flower to her nose. She gently inhaled its aroma before he squeezed the flower into his hands and gave her the juice to drink.

"Wow," the girl exclaimed. "What is this place?"

Jack had an idea and guided her with his intent alone.

"Come with me," he then insisted, grabbing the girls hand and sweeping her away. He knew he had to be quick. The others realised what he was doing with his image creating, they just didn't fully understand why.

"Look across that valley. Look at the mountain and the trees reflecting on the beautiful calm lake. Have you ever seen a mountain before?" he asked the girl, without an apology for the crude rhetoric offered.

"Of course I have, we have mountains too."

"Yes, but have you ever seen one? Really seen one? Do you also have lakes there?" he added cheekily.

"Of course we have lakes," she snarled disappointedly, after hoping for help and receiving hopeless quips.

"And have you ever seen one?"

"Yes, I have looked at a …."

"Looking and seeing are not the same thing," he said. "Now close your eyes." A river teaming with vibrancy flowed swiftly past them.

"Right you can open them now," he said, admiring the work of his own mind. "What can you see? What do you know about the colours? Look how the rock sits so still against the movement of the water. What does the lightness and darkness represent for you? Can you hear the silence inside the noise of the flow? Can you see how the softness of the water has carved the rock away? Have you ever seen a river?" he asked again.

"I think I understand what you are saying," she said, all signs of her previous acrimony abated.

"You mustn't ever think you understand something. You must always know you understand. Thinking only ever gets in the way. Quick look up," Jack remarked.

She witnessed a brilliant sunrise, proudly peeping over a snow capped hill.

"Bet you've never seen one of those before?"

The girl didn't answer this time.

"What about oceans and rainbows, or listening to the birds singing as the sun rises? Have you ever seen the moon reflecting on a clear pond, or smelt the scent of spring as you walk across a freshly mown field? Surely you must have run barefoot along a golden beach with the sun on your back before diving into a clear blue ocean? And you must have held a new born baby and felt the wonder of that tiny miracle? Are you certain you have nothing to go back for?"

"Yes, yes and yes," she cried. "I have done and seen all of those things, but they never meant very much to me. Seeing that you know so much, tell me how can that be?"

"Because you were not alive in that moment of course, your attention was elsewhere, probably somewhere in the past or the future. Paradise and hell are in all places, here and there, this world and yours, and all in between. You are merely travelling between them. And what's more, every second you are choosing which one you will experience. You are choosing between light and dark, fear and love, pleasure and pain. Heaven and hell are as real as you make them. But in truth they are both illusion. Understanding and awareness is your real measure of pain or pleasure."

She looked down once more and saw the doctors working on her body. She was certain now she had to go back but was still afraid of the pain. As she lifted her head she saw a figure slowly approaching. The figure got closer and she focused on the features appearing through the veil like mist. Suddenly she thought she knew him. Then, she knew she knew him.

"Daddy," she screamed, and ran to him, and screamed some more. Running into those open arms she appreciated for the first time in her life the power of a heartfelt hug. She melted into his body. It felt as real as anything she had ever experienced, the two fusing almost into one.

"You must go back sweetness, now is not your time. We will meet again before you know it. Take the lessons you have learned and use them to teach others, and remember you are never alone, never. The love you have felt here is with you always."

One more enthusiastic hug was stolen from the father she thought she had lost forever when she was just eleven years old. No words were necessary. Her whole life had changed in the space of a few minutes. She would never fear death again and she knew for certain she would return to this incredible place once more and he would be still be here, waiting for her.

She walked over to where Jack was standing, threw her arms out and pulled him in close, staggered at how much love he had shown to a complete stranger.

She felt herself being pulled down towards the Earth and towards her broken body, still lying in the coldness of the theatre room. She was scared, of course she was, but also exited at the chance to live the rest of her life without fear, determined to see the magic in what she had previously seen as mundane.

She smiled as she visualised everyone who knew her saying how unlucky she had been to have such a terrible accident. She had learned something valuable about good luck and bad luck.

Jack was delighted with the outcome too. He put his arms around the girl's father and held him. There was a great love between them already and that simple meeting developed into a continuous connection. It's always like that once you realise that everyone and everything comes from the same source, very easy to feel love and empathy for everyone and everything you encounter. But I have to sneak this controversial statement in, it is imperative. All that coming and going is not necessary, not really, it is mind caught in a trap, that's all. There, all done now.

The friends gathered around Jack and praised his speed of thought before drifting to the pasture once more, back in the moment to bathe in the beauty and reflect on the little adventure with the girl.

5

JUSTICE

Not all justice takes place in one lifetime.

IT'S A GIRL, the cards all said so, the cards which occupied every flat surface in the living room, postponing Friday's dusting, encouraging ongoing untidiness, and smugly watching the old news papers pass them, heading unmercifully for the re-cycle bin. Fifty seven cards in total, including the six duplicates, and not one of them said "Welcome Joseph."

Families and friends gathered to see the old spirit wrapped in new baby skin and new baby blankets, a great joy for everyone concerned.

The name Annabelle had been painstakingly selected and she would undoubtedly wear it quite naturally in the months ahead.

Pass the parcel commenced, hurriedly from one amazed person to the other. The love they felt for her was instant, yet would prove to be eternal. And the child like way they spoke to her did seem strange from the universal angle, especially considering all the wisdom and experience she has. But this is how it goes and the laws are known pre hand, begin anew; clean slate, all idea of purpose and plan lost in transit.

Annabelle's new family lived in a region of Ireland called County Mayo, just near the coast, in a wonderfully quaint town named Mulranny. It was a peaceful and unhurried town, not much happening, almost horse and cartish.

The family linage had been traced back to before the sixteenth century and they had been in and around County Mayo since the times of the great Grace O Malley.

Tragically some of the family had to leave this picturesque part of the world in the mid 1800s, having no means of survival during the potato famine, a famine engineered by the English government. In sheer desperation, but full cosmic agreement, they had made the trip to Dublin, grabbing only the things they could carry, including their children. From there they sailed to Liverpool in England, before making the short trip up to Manchester, with whispered promises of employment.

Manchester in the 1800s was an ugly, evil and dangerous place to exist. With its narrow filthy streets, sprawling railway viaducts, toxic canals and a thick black cloud covering the city, it would have been difficult to design a better version of hell on Earth.

In many ways it was a disposable city built mostly for trade, and the buildings, vibrant and bursting with life one moment, were quickly left to corrode after their purpose had been fulfilled.

In the 1830s it was estimated that eighteen thousand people lived in the cellars of Manchester, one third of which were Irish. Most of the cellars were pitch black, damp, and with no ventilation. The majority were single rooms without light, sanitation or running water. Hardly any of the streets had drainage or sewage and as a result the floors of the cellars were often formed by human waste. It was not unknown for up to twelve people to be sharing one of these rooms.

Bronchitis, pneumonia, asthma and influenza murdered any hope of optimism and the average life expectancy dropped to fifteen at one point, while the national average was forty.

Manchester was also a very violent city during this period and the desperate Irish were usually on the receiving end. Imagine the utter despair of leaving the paradise of County Mayo for the squalor of those streets. They would certainly have been forgiven for assuming there was no justice. This horrific history was now connected to the Annabelle family tree, the dismal software of genetic squalor efficiently downloaded on to Annabelle's hard drive.

How the Irish remain one of the nicest and simplistic races on Earth is a mystery. Their ability to forgive and forget is remarkable.

6

RESPONSIBILITY

Yes you did choose to be born.

Idle days trickled by and nonchalantly formed the structures of weeks and months, the slow pace of a life gently moulding its tranquillity on to Annabelle's psyche.

Things would obviously become a little difficult in later years due to the path she had chosen. Her mother's failing health would ensure the role of a carer would need fulfilling. Lack of money would also show its destructive side as her dad, emotionally derailed, would have to spend more time at home helping out, his part time shopkeeper's income barely covering the basics. Perfect!

Fortunately whenever the money did dry up it only succeeded in making them pull together more, a brave attempt at compensating with love when currency felt like the obvious king.

Annabelle would never moan about her life, much preferring to get on with it the best she could. Others, in the same circumstances may have spent it dwelling on the negative, even suggesting that they didn't choose to be born and weren't responsible for their life, but Annabelle always played her deck the best she could, regardless of the dealer or the cards dealt.

Realising that we are fully responsible for our life and everyone who comes into it, is a giant step towards accessing the full potential of what's on offer. To accept that all the bad things in our life are there because we attracted or agreed to them means we can stop blaming others and get on with creating a more positive and powerful life. This simple realisation will turn any life around. Go on, give it a try, I don't make the rules up.

Annabelle's father was a wonderful, gentle, and surprisingly wise man, surprisingly because he didn't know it himself, measuring as the human tends to, only in certificates of the intellect and so never developing an articulation of his natural wisdom.

His features were soft, warm and inviting, every part of his face emanating kindness. He had the endearing habit of laughing at the slightest of things, infecting anyone in his company with his ability to see the sensational in the mundane, the extraordinary in the ordinary. As comfortable as he was in company he was equally happy keeping himself to himself. Happier if truth be known.

Roy lived life in a very simplistic way; he upset no-one and disturbed nothing. His house had nothing frivolous, technical or superfluous in it. Two simple chairs were pulled up round the open fire, two welsh dresser chairs for guests occupied the wall opposite the window. On the back wall, the opposite one to the fire place was an old, if not antique, display cabinet. Its decorative strips of wood had long since given up impressing and a pane of the patterned glass exposed a crack from a 1990 celebration marking the end of the Thatcher era, when a champagne cork took an uncanny deflection, which by no means detracted from the euphoria Roy experienced at her demise, but did show similar ruthless tendencies to that of an Argentinean bound torpedo, as it located the defenceless and utterly innocent pane of glass. Apart from that it was the perfect thing for displaying old glasses, out of date spirits and empty spectacle cases.

In their tiny back garden he lovingly nurtured his plants and always made sure the birds were well fed. He harboured no longing for success as other people measured it and seemed to be one of a rare breed who didn't need material objects to make him happy. Some people just seem to have the knowledge that real happiness can not be bought, most, unfortunately don't. I imagine that you yourself will even know people who strive for the latest top of the range car, or the most expensive watch or biggest house in the neighbourhood. And I imagine you will observe, only a month after, the car sits filthy on the drive, the watch is barely looked at and the huge house is not quite big enough for the deluded occupant. So the hunt begins again to satisfy an ego that can never be satisfied.

Roy however was not of this mindset. He had mastered the art of being happy with very little. Many of his belongings were made by himself, recycled offerings from anything he had no further use for.

A broken table for instance would be dismantled and re-appear as a set of shelves. When his kettle stopped functioning it turned up in the garden, hand painted and offering the perfect home for a grateful Grevillea. And in the doing of these acts of sincere simplicity can surely be found the measure of true happiness. To be completely engrossed in the moments that join together and make twenty four hours in a day is paradoxically the only ingredients you will need for the seemingly complex pursuit of achieving true success and happiness.

Roy's neighbour, who never quite understood him, often spoke to him about his own quest for happiness, stubbornly waiting in that long queue of naivety, waiting and hoping for his chance to be happy, believing it would come with the arrival of a holiday, when he had paid off his debts, or when he finally retired.

He told Roy one afternoon, I remember it well, over the fence made from a derelict shed, that he had ordered a top of the range television, due to be delivered a week on Friday. He said he would be happy when it arrived. Roy laughed to himself at the very idea that happiness could be hunted down and caught like a butterfly in a net.

After the conversation Roy stayed in his back yard to feed the birds, chopped some wood and spent the evening sanding down an old wooden chair he had found on the Wednesday flea market. When he had finished the sanding, he spent forty five minutes looking at the way it had worn over time and pondering how many people had sat on it during its life. He then thought about tomorrow and how he would varnish the chair and return it to its former glory. What a day tomorrow would be.

Annabelle knew how lucky she was to be brought up by this gentle and loving man. However long they were together in this life would not be the end of their story. She knew instinctively their lives, love, and experiences would stretch out forever across an infinite universe without end.

If learning lessons and expressing love are the reasons we come to Earth, and each time we are in difficult situations we act with humility and compassion to improve the circumstances of our next incarnation, then Annabelle and Roy were in the process of creating an incredible next time around.

7

SPIRIT GUIDES

What unswerving dedication, tirelessly working behind the scenes, supporting, guiding and assisting you wherever they can, and quite often without a single thank you in a whole lifetime.

Back at the pasture Delmore was in deep discussion with his friends, including the great guide Soran, drafted in to look over the circumstances of his next journey.

"I believe you are looking for a way to express your genius creativity, have you got a lot of it?" Soran asked by thought, redundant of larynx and diaphragm.

Delmore thought briefly about the answer, ignoring the invitation to stoke the embers of his long gone ego.

"I would never consider myself a genius, it's a huge passion though, and yes, if I'm creating here, I may as well carry it with me."

"Well, if I have done my job properly, and I think I have, we may well have a good ride out for you," Soran added, a signal of don't-ask-me-any-more subtly sent.

"Tell me more," Delmore asked, signal ignored.

"Frankly, I would rather not talk about it; we must wait for the linear line of Earth time to unravel," he said, bringing the others in the conversation and bringing the instalment to an end.

His friends knew he would be saying goodbye soon, sadness would be certain, but the knowledge that goodbyes are not for ever and merely mean "see you soon" to those who know the path of unbroken existence was a welcome balancer.

Soran was a very old friend of Delmore's, many times connected and the agreement to oversee his incarnation was an easy decision for him. But more of Delmore later, you must remain sequential Conrad, none of your cosmic illogic.

I say sequential because it was actually Kitty who was next to go, a great opportunity had arisen, I say arisen, but mean a diligently selected opportunity shown to her by one of her own assigned guides. A couple in North Morocco had been tracked down, Google earthed, you might prefer, (I've done a little research) wealthy and influential and travelling extensively in pursuit of their passion of acquiring great works of art.

They resided in a spectacular riad on the edge of the city of Tetouan. Opportunities for travel and freedom, if Kitty accepted this particular life, would be stacked high. She certainly liked the look of all this did our Kitty, great excitement unashamedly displayed at the prospect of prosperity. And as they looked further down that time line they could also see that another child would be born into the family.

"This is perfect Robert, you could be following me soon," she told him, pulling on his shirt tails for emphasis.

"Can you imagine it, me and you back on the old planet once more?" he replied, with equal delight.

"Things are changing, always changing; we need more than a handful of inner strength to keep on top," Delmore said, before speeding off; an invitation to follow flickering in his cosmic trails.

He hovered momentarily, creating the journey with thought before pursuing it with movement, outwards through time and space. The others followed closely, pure joy in the weightlessness, not a trace of worry or fear, dancing and merging with the other light beings they encountered on the way, tailoring their imagination to a powerful peak. They immersed themselves in absolute freedom and bliss before being guided back to the calmness of the pasture, watching as Delmore left once more, slowly and reflectively this time.

"What an incredible journey," beamed Annie.

"I will miss this freedom when I eventually leave," replied Jack, accidentally bringing a weight back into the situation. "I just wish it could be like this down there instead of, well, I mean everything is so slow and heavy?"

"There are many reasons for it," Delmore said, reappearing instantly next to Jack with his explanation.

"Gravity is one of them, time is another. As you know time works in lines down there, past, present, and future so clearly defined, yet elsewhere in the universe it's all happening in the now. You know when we concentrate on a place or a person or feeling, well it happens in an instant. On Earth when we try to create something with our mind it can take a day, a week, or even years before you see it manifest. It's a much slower learning process. That's a good thing for people who always think negative thoughts and only see outcomes in the format of tragedy, as they would be swamped with bad situations piling up and paralysing them, a scrap yard of negativity they would live in. With Earth's slower vibration however, they have more time to deal with the results of their thoughts. But for the more positive, dynamic and creative, well I guess it can be a drag. Of course Jack, you know it is possible to override the process somewhat, but you have to throw out those outdated belief patterns and allow only thoughts that support your story of who you want to be."

Jack listened pensively, returning serve only when he was sure of the height of the net.

"That is the most exciting aspect of incarnating for me. Knowing that when, or if you get to that point of realisation you can literally write your life story and watch it unfold. Throwing out the lie that you have to accept the story that others have written for you and becoming anything that you choose to become. It can be a long journey though, to realise it's your own life."

They concluded the conversation by giggling at the madness of their future earthling mindset.

8

ENLIGHTENMENT

Maybe enlightenment is just having the knowledge that it's unattainable through merely wanting to attain it.

The moment for Kitty to leave had arrived, and once more on Planet Earth a new human form was being created. How incredible to think that this goes on thousands of times a day, every day, all over the world, and that thousands of spirits are waiting to enter, choosing a body suit to wear for a few years, whether four years or ninety four years, it matters not where time matters not.

And each time there is the potential to refine and develop a bit more in a journey that will ultimately return us all to the source of which lies pure love. Not a bad existence when you see it like that is it? Then again, it could just be that you get squeezed out of a toothpaste tube and land in the street where you were born. I suppose you can only see which one resonates as a truth for you, both maybe possible.

So, the journey itself, whether you go for the cosmic theory or the Colgate one, is unfortunately, usually accompanied by the futile search that so many lifetimes are wasted on. That search being the one for happiness, for enlightenment and for love, and futile because we are already all of it, pure love dressed in a body suit having an experience to add to all the experiences we've had in a universal journey with no end.

Our wonderful Kitty was well prepared for her next instalment of that journey. A body had been made and that body needed a driver to operate it through its life on Earth, and she, the elated recipient of the great news; had the added bonus of being joined by Robert, making the trip even more appealing.

Delmore appeared and held her close, silently wishing her well. Jack and Florence came and held Kitty too, promising once more to be waiting whenever she came home.

"Don't forget we will be at the pasture when you arrive. See you in a moment," Florence mused, teasing time's fragile framework.

Robert walked towards Kitty and offered her his hand.

"I can't believe we will both be together in Morocco and remember none of this." Kitty said, holding him tightly.

"I know, I know, the world has its strange ways and everyone there will do their best for us whilst gently manipulating us into their reality, a reality which will not encourage us to be the multi dimensional beings we know we are. We must try to remember though."

Delmore could only nod his head as they prepared for her departure, watching Kitty surrender her spirit in the name of development, before sadly leaving them all behind.

"Kitty is in Morocco now," Robert said resolutely. He reflected a moment, then said. "How lucky we are to have these extraordinary experiences."

And for me, it's off to Morocco too; bring you up to spec as they say.

THREE EARTH YEARS LATER

It was a particularly hot day in the middle of July as Kitty, now a three year old girl named Falak, waited excitedly for the arrival of her new baby brother. He came in the early hours of that hot and humid evening, born in the lush bedroom of their wonderful home, the long anticipation finally over.

They lovingly washed and dressed him, worrying about the weight of cotton wool and positively paranoid about press studs. Eventually they brought him over to where Falak was sitting and held him carefully on her lap.

"This is Latif," the proud father announced.

"Is this really my own baby brother?" she giggled, eyes transfixed and burning pure love into the soul behind the tiny frame.

She held him for a while longer before the father, Hacham, returned the new born to rest with his mother. He then carried Falak up to their rooftop garden. A gentle breeze blew down from the Rif Mountains, carrying with it a mixture of the scent of flowers from around the neighbourhood and charcoal from the burning barbeques outside. The stars were shimmering in the clear night sky and in the distance dogs were barking for reasons no-one ever knew.

In those few moments, as he gazed at his beautiful daughter, he grasped the true essence of joy, a joy that would have been no less intense had he been in a tiny bed-sit in Tangiers.

The one thing his wealth would buy however was the opportunity to spend almost all their time watching their children growing up. They were able to stay at home with Latif and Falak without the necessary sacrifice of the whip cracking, slave driving system we call work.

If abundance was the goal of Kitty's incarnation, she was on a sure-fire winner. There were copious amounts of love, freedom, and opportunities to see the diversity and incredulousness of this world we often begrudgingly trudge through.

Latif and Falak soon became inseparable. They bonded beyond everyone's expectations, people constantly commenting on their closeness. In fact Falak was a little over protective of her brother, but no-one interfered, cuteness over correction won out every time.

Hacham and his wife Zahra were very knowledgeable in their field, very knowledgeable, and this knowledge would be genetically and of course through the influence of their environment, passionately passed on to the children. And as they grew, bones bending to Bosch, skin stretching to Seurat, that knowledge became a love for painting too, being surrounded by great works of art was understandably a great influence in their lives.

They had many friends in Tetouan; they had many friends throughout the world, all of them made welcome in their home. Generous with their wealth they always strived to help out others who were not so fortunate. They never tried to accumulate money and as it came in, so it went out, creating a flow that seemed to work for the good of everyone. Instinct told them that by clinging on to their wealth they would block the natural flow of energy. A fact many rich people just don't get. In fact, many poor too.

As I mentioned before, travel was an integral part of their lives, they were confident travellers and the fear of foreign soil had long since perished.

Now then, as much as they did love their worldly jaunts, and I tell you they really did, it was equalled with comparative ease, by a five minute walk to their local medina. The smells and the sounds of that bustling market square had left giant imprints on their five senses. Nothing stimulates the senses like a Moroccan market you know.

9

PREPERATION

Whether you are coming or going it is imperative you are prepared. Tie up your loose ends, forgive your enemies and thank your friends. You can never know what's around the corner.

Delmore was keeping himself busy, studying the effects of light and dark, creating colours and images for his own amusement and the absolute amazement of everyone else. This is the way he chose to spend his last moments here, typical Delmore.

Annie and Jack were relaxing by a dramatic aqua blue lake when Delmore thought his way over to them.

"Where is Florence?" he asked.

"She is right behind you now," Annie chuckled, surprised by her instant arrival. Florence was there too, with friends of her own.

"I've come to say goodbye," Delmore announced. "Off to collect another feather for my cosmic cap."

"We will see you in no time," Annie assured, playing once more with its irrelevance.

"Of course you will, of that we can be certain. Yes time, the great illusion of the Planet Earth," he sighed. "If I can keep my perception clear and my mind still, well, who knows, timeless on Earth, what do you think? Some have you know."

"Please try Delmore," pleaded Florence, the change in tone indicating a more serious under current than the one displayed. "Then when you are in that state we can meet in the place that floats between both worlds and never really leave each other."

"I don't believe we ever do Florence. We just become so obsessed with the body and physicality we forget we have a "connected to all things spirit" too, and not just a body with maybe a little spirit inside. I hope I don't get too embroiled in the appearance of my Earth body, you know like they do down there, obsessed with looking beautiful, even paying to have it altered, to have it more pleasing to the eye, fighting natural aging processes in a futile effort to somehow prolong the life of the body at all costs. Save the body and ignore the spirit.

Hey, I won't be going if I carry on like this, just a spirit wearing a temporary suit, that's all I'll be. Anyway, whatever happens to me I know I will be back home one day, and hopefully, well, I'm almost certain I'll bring some good stories with me."

His focus suddenly shifted, an increase in the resonance of his vibrations was clearly noticeable to Annie, the sure-fire precursor to transformation. She knew she was losing him.

"Goodbye and good luck Delmore."

Delmore had a last glimpse of his world before he felt the pull of the Earth and descended through tunnels of light, twisting through the helix of time before landing in the womb of new creation.

So that was how Delmore left the spirit world, more or less. He had chosen his new incarnation with great care and much guidance; now all that was left was to fill out a number of days with purpose, to live it to his highest possible potential and allow the universe to express itself through his new vehicle. Not as easy as I make it sound, I know, but I offer you the essence anyway.

10

ADVENTURE

With a cup of coffee, a map, and a heart full of courage you can create something truly spectacular.

The family, assiduously chosen by Soran and Delmore were natural creators in the musical field. He had been around them before in various relationships and oaths made long ago were now being given a platform of reality to be honoured from.

The support and encouragement that would eventually allow him absolute creative accomplishment was their biggest commitment to him.

There was another reason for him choosing this particular life too. He had taken the opportunity to be re-united with an old friend, an old friend of many shared incarnations, and an old friend who was still living in the same earthly form as when Delmore last left him. The desire to go back had always been a strong one, the manner in which they were cruelly separated modifying and finally engulfing his feelings.

Now, his creative yearning had led him to a small village in the South of Spain. Narrow, dusty streets with bright white houses in clinging clusters hung perilously but hopefully to the side of a huge hill. The fact they had stood there for hundreds of years did nothing to allay the fear and anguish suffered by the casual observer. Their ability to look as though they would topple any minute always showed prominence.

Delmore's house was modest with few luxuries, but no different to any of the others there. It's my guess, as cosmic story teller mind, and not property investor, but my guess would be that it would be classed as a poor village. Yet, delighted as I was to discover, no-one ever went hungry there, or did without essentials, community spirit in full flow being the unrivalled success of any village.

The day he was born, a late Wednesday afternoon, siesta time, many of the inhabitants of the village made the climb up to his house at the top of the hill, leaving small gifts and big wishes to the new arrival they had named Juan.

His two brothers and his sister were delighted with the latest addition to their family, begging their mother to let Juan share their bedroom, when he moved on from the Moses basket of course, the gesture being a benevolent, if not slightly ambitious one, spacious bedrooms were not in abundance there in that village. Things were going to get cramped for certain and adaptations were imminent.

Fortunately the house had a very large roof terrace which looked to mountains one way and down across the village the other. A great deal of their days were spent on that roof, and many evenings too.

There was a cooker, barbecue area, fridge and storage cabinets, a makeshift kitchen under a corrugated tin roof. The mother had all she needed to cater for them up there, and if she did ever find herself short of anything, she had the ability to project her voice in such a way she could converse with neighbours from across similar rooftops, asking to borrow an item of cutlery or missing ingredients for lunch. In fact all her neighbours had acquired the talent of voice throwing; they shared stories and kept up with all the village's happenings by the sheer power of a well developed lung capacity.

Long summer nights were passed playing instruments and singing to the stars, forcing them to come out and listen.

The family regularly made the pilgrimage through the narrow streets, winding their way up to the church on the opposite hill. It was a very charming church set in a wonderful location, sitting elegantly in the tranquillity of lovingly maintained gardens, the perfect environment to facilitate the contemplation of life, perfect also for filling in those gaps left by endless summer days. Almost everyone in the village had family members or friends buried in the church grounds and not a week went by without them visiting the small shrines which contained the ashes that were once the bodies they shared the thick and thins of life with.

Flowers and small gifts were devoutly placed, aching regrets over bodies long gone, tears shed over a spirit who was somewhere in the universe laughing like a child.

At midnight each evening the lights next to the palm tree in the grounds of the church went out, effectively closing the curtains on the village for a great silence to reign.

And this serene simplicity provided the backdrop for the whole of Juan's childhood, a slow and gentle existence with all traces of stress melted away by the ferociousness of the sun. It would offer him the chance to discover himself without the usual distractions a bustling city would enforce. But even where the serene is supreme, life and its necessary challenges will seek you out. Juan would find out this soon enough.

A FEW MORE YEARS LATER

The sun was setting over the bow of the ship, free falling to the back of the world. Falak and Latif were standing on the upper deck, the island of Cuba fading behind them and the lights on the headline of the island in front, just appearing.

"There it is, Jamaica," Falak squealed. "Won't it be great?"

"I hope so," said her younger brother, trying to fit his head through the gap in two bars, the way only a boy would, with total absence of consequence. Mum and dad came and joined them, perhaps in the nick of time. They looked up to a sky full of stars which served as a weather forecast for the day after. The night was a warm one and it felt good to be outside.

"Soon be there now," dad said, tightening his grip on them both.

"Straight to the hotel and straight to bed I think," he added with unconvincing authority.

"Can we have a swim if the pool is still open, or in the sea dad?"

"Yes, yes, of course, I'm certain it will all still be open," he lied; certain everywhere would be quite the opposite.

The ship rocked from side to side, lazily plotting its course, its nose resolutely resigned to Jamaica.

They stood quietly watching the orange lights at the port of Ocho Rios growing bigger and brighter.

Jamaica had been selected, whimsically as always by their father, a painting on a cluttered restaurant wall in Casablanca being enough of a reason for them to travel across the world to meet the young artist responsible. He would see his collection of art work, buy the ones he liked and use his influence in the art world to lift the profile of the struggling artist. That was the idea anyway.

Falak and Latif's life so far had been just like this. The wealth of their parents had bought them opportunities to experience many great things. More importantly it had spared them the poverty mentality that nearly always accompanies less fortunate families, so creating a very difficult cycle to break. Fortunately we all have a share of both ends of the spectrum and all cannot be judged in one lifetime. Of course affluence does not mean immunity from life's hardships; they had their ups and downs like everybody else, deaths of relatives and friends, fall outs with each other, problems with school bullies, general misdemeanours and such. In fact Falak had suffered regularly at the hands of some of her school colleagues, envious of her predicament and focused on cruelty, safe in their numbers, always. Yes they had tried and failed, in the long run, to make her existence a miserable one.

One day, frail and emotional, Falak had asked her father why it was that even if you are really nice and never hurt anyone that bad things can still happen to you. His answer provided the necessary comfort his wounded daughter needed.

"Well Falak," he began, gentle tone for soothing purposes, nicely selected. "Just because a person is nice and wouldn't hurt another doesn't mean the universe will spare them the opportunity of learning to grow through the gift of problems and challenges, it wouldn't dream of leaving you out," he told her. It was a sentiment which had always stayed with her, a possible future "my father once said" kind of quote, handed down to the struggling spirits of generations yet to come.

The ship finally banged and clanged to a halt, it's failing tannoy system announcing the arrival for the absolute oblivious. Mum and dad were cuddled up to their children who had faces pressed against the window, trying to get a feel of Jamaica before they had stepped on its soil.

After the delayed docking, chaotic customs and a terrifying taxi ride the fatigued but relieved family put their bags down in the lobby of Negril's finest hotel. A telepathic vote saw bed the unanimous victor, the law of non resistance sweetly applied.

Morning came much too quickly for mum and dad, enviously watching their refreshed children running straight from their beds to the sand, wild expressions and a few thousand small footprints left in the sand, the subtle clues of sheer ecstasy.

So impressed by this simple pleasure, they made it a daily pre breakfast event, a wonderful welcome to the morning from a world without worry. This morning beach ritual was the way they got to know the shop owners, the water sports enthusiasts, and even the marijuana dealers on that stretch who had the most polite and inoffensive manner of trying to ply their trade. They always had time for a chat and a spot of philosophy even when it was clearly obvious they would not make a dollar with this family.

It was on the advice of one of these dealers as a matter of fact, that they took a trip to the river falls and spent a still talked about day amongst amazingly lush terrain, made possible by the extreme diversity of the rainy season coupled with hours of incredible sunshine, a paradise which no amount of imagination could improve on.

They were helped with great kindness by the locals who knew how to get them in the water and back out with minimum fuss and virtually no risk. They swung on ropes, sailed down river in huge rubber tyres and ate lunch grown on trees, in an afternoon taster of how those Jamaicans lived each day, an absence of money in their pockets yet paradoxically the richest people on the planet.

"One love" blasted out of crackling speakers which nestled in the doors of a battered Ford Cortina on the journey back to Negril. They drove through shanty towns consisting of wooden shacks carefully squeezed into any gap of land the landowner would permit. How they survived the hurricane season remained a nailed down secret to all tourists, available only to those with Jamaican blood running through their veins.

Through a dust filled window that wouldn't wind down they saw groups of people hanging around the houses, sitting on the porches or idly watching the world go by, philosophers of great stature without recognition. As far as possessions went they would carry the label poor, yet next to their falling down homes was an abundance of orange trees, banana trees, and many other fruits growing in profusion. They plucked off these exotic offerings whenever the urge took them and with an afternoon hammock or a luxurious beach never too far away, the boundaries of rich and poor became very blurred.

Hacham found his artist living above a shop selling fruit and vegetables in a town three miles up the coast. The shop sat just a few yards back from the beach, nestled among palm trees, two abandoned cars, a home made porch swing, and an adjoining shop selling hardware. He confidently introduced himself and went about transforming a relatively unknown artist into a highly respected and world famous figure with a natural ease. Worn out shoes would soon be exchanged, holey clothes replaced, and all material yearnings satisfied as talent now traded with currency. Another life brought to life by the acute observations of a man doing what his heart loved to do.

He had arrived at this privileged position through fierce focus and an appreciation of art impossible to suppress. There was nothing more he wanted than to spend his life surrounded by artists and paintings.

Ironically he had been brought up with a complete lack of luxury and the cruel anchor of poverty rooted his early existence. The idea of living abundantly was an absent one for Hacham as a child, yet somehow, through doing only what made his heart sing he was now living a life that was full of purpose and pleasure. So there you go, go and do only what makes your heart sing.

11

TEACHERS

Life's most inspiring lessons are seldom taught in the classroom. Tramps, vagabonds, alcoholics and village idiots can be wonderful teachers if you can be humble enough to listen.

Juan attended a standard school at the bottom of the village, seldom enjoying, more often enduring a basic education. He was a keen and attentive learner in general, but he had developed a questioning and somewhat challenging response to what his teachers tried to teach him. He seemed to have an inherent understanding that there was more to his existence, and that of his world, than was being offered. Of course he would think that.

It had also become apparent to his parents that he was very different to his brothers and sisters. He carried a lust for life they had not recognised in his peers, undoubtedly they were proud, but worry was never more than a bemused teacher's phone call away. Curious and intense with his focus he was forever expanding his knowledge, usually being found behind the cover of a book, opening his covetous mind further, as his parents pondered the fact he may be losing it completely.

He had already, through sheer focus and brutal determination, become the best musician in the family. Not being content to just play time honoured songs from the Spanish folk genre; he had even taken to writing songs himself. Sure enough he enjoyed the intimacy of those long evenings on the terrace and the harmony he achieved with his fellow musicians and family members, yet he couldn't deny the satisfaction when one of his own compositions came together, original arrangements always deeply rooted in the melodic, and his inquisitive mind harnessed to offer his theories and beliefs in the message riddled content of the lyrics.

Just after his fourteenth birthday, Juan, his two brothers and his father took a fantastic trip inland to the mountains. The winding road that led them there lazily snaked its way through Las Alpujarras, invigorating Juan with its rugged natural beauty. He anticipated big things and new adventures on his stay in the mountains, life changing he even thought to himself, grounded only by his brothers who moaned round the bends and groaned on the straights.

They drove through a hippy type town named Orjiva, proudly parading more misfits than a travelling circus. Healers, dealers, musicians, artists and performers all wandered the streets with carefree abandon. Juan made a mental note to return one day. These misfits to the narrow norm of society fitted right in with Juan's wonky world.

A descending petrol gauge and an ascending temperature gauge influenced their next stop, an almost derelict garage the welcome sanctuary to feed their old Renault with necessary nutrients before climbing further upwards.

The scenery soon began to open up, teasing and tricking their eyes into paying more attention before the mountains soared and declared themselves "Kings of the vista." Climbing further still they passed through the first village in the Poqueira Ravine, a beautiful, although slightly touristy affair called Pampiniera. A couple of kilometres more revealed the pivotal sign for Methina Fondales. A sharp right turn brought them to a tiny, restful village; the sound of the squealing tyres on the dusty hot road seemed massively exaggerated. Dad stopped the car outside a small bar and Juan read the name out loud. "Bar Aljibe."

The family unfolded and stretched their crumpled bodies out, automatically breathing deeper as if it would be rude not to. Juan felt a strange feeling of familiarity. He looked around, fully expecting to see something he would recognise.

As they trudged up the gravel path towards Aljibe they adjusted their step to one of exaggerated lightness, fearing they would wake the village's inhabitants if they didn't. Apart from one young man sitting outside, contemplating life through the remnants of an espresso coffee, they saw nobody.

Quickly making necessary eye adjustments from bright sunlight to semi darkness they checked for any form of life, scanning the place with tourist trepidation. At the corner table a man was sitting alone casually writing in a small notebook. The father walked towards him but he continued writing without looking up.

"Excuse me, would you be able to tell me where I can find the house Los Monteros?" he chanced.

The man took a moment to acknowledge the request before proceeding to put his pen in his top pocket and his little book in a bag at his side, the delay in answering causing the father to doubt his sanity.

"Yes indeed I know of it," he finally said. "Come, I will escort you to the house with the view of the mountain. A mountain which is surely going to change your life I may add."

He led the way out of the bar and together they took the two minute walk. Los Monteros looked tiny from the outside, yet like most village houses it was deceptively spacious once their feet were through the door. They got their first glance of the mountain as they approached the house.

"Thank you," the father shouted to the man, who had already begun his return trip.

"Giving thanks is easy," he replied. "Being truly grateful is an art form."

He gave a wave and took off at a sprint that had little relevance to his age.

An intrigued but slightly suspicious father warned his sons to keep away from the strange man. Juan made another mental note to do the opposite.

"Wait here boys, I'll go back and bring the car," he said, still shaking his head at what he had just witnessed.

The boys felt jubilation in being released from the confines of a three door hatchback, running on the spot and making woo hoo sounds being the chosen celebration. A middle aged, friendly faced lady appeared from inside the house, ending the celebrations with unwelcome sobriety.

"Welcome children, surely you have not come alone?" she asked, already finding glasses and filling them for the guests.

"We are waiting for our father," José said, dutifully accepting the glass thrust in his hand.

"Come in, come in, let me show you around, I know you will like it here. We have the most wonderful flowers in springtime; you are a little late for that though. You must visit the nearby villages too; they are very pretty although this particular one does happen to be my favourite, I hope you won't get bored," she said, without pause, dispensing two more glasses of water without mention of glass, water, or thirst. Before they had the chance to engage with her, the car was back and they set about bringing their belongings in.

They would be staying in Methina Fondales for two weeks, a rare opportunity for them to do some walking and to take time to be together, booked on a whim by their father as he momentarily felt them being stolen from him by the panic of puberty. He wanted to slow time down and savour the preciousness of family life. The peace and quiet would be his chief ally in achieving this.

Their home village was certainly peaceful enough, in the main, but in July and August peace was the last thing you were likely to get. With the children off school and never entering their bedrooms till after midnight, the noise of their giddiness soared and found thermals to circle the whole village on. Dogs yapped across terraces to each other and young boys on under powered scooters, naively believing that the more noise they made the more impressed girls would be, took the trophy with "evening irritant" engraved on it. Even the beauty of nature seemed overstated as the birds joined forces with the insects to reach a crescendo of expression and give the dogs more reason to bark.

Things were different in those mountains though, and Juan felt the power of penetrating silence.

After the owner left them to settle in, they walked through to the back of the house which opened out to display a patio with an incredible view of the mountains. They would spend their first and every subsequent evening sat out there, the silence only broken by the occasional owl cry, or the arguing and general boisterousness of his two elder brothers, José and David.

The stillness and vastness of those mountains instantly captivated Juan. He would watch them change colours at different times of the day, and he acquired a new way of seeing, same eyes but different outlook, fierce concentration and intense focus on the colours which finally materialised in an overwhelming urge to paint. A necessity to capture a unique part of the world he lived in, something personal to him, something no-one else could see.

These kaleidoscopic impulses were new feelings for Juan. He felt raw excitement race through his blood and recognised its seriousness, the new challenge, the idea of going from knowing nothing about a subject to seeing how far he could take it, another lens to view his incredible world through. He also knew David, José, and his father weren't seeing the same thing as him, even though they were looking at the same thing.

Juan went to bed that night and dreamed about painting. He saw vivid colours and was recreating them freely, the owner of psychedelic swirls and pretty patterns.

The morning after they all woke much later than their intended agreement, the absolute silence allowing them the bliss of unbroken sleep. They ate breakfast out on the terrace, it was already sunny and Juan noted how the morning changed the colours of the mountains, greens giving way to yellows and later to purples as the sun blessed it with its light. He knew he was on a new path.

After breakfast the four of them went on their first exploration out of the village. Five minutes saw them leave one and enter another, the old weathered sign post informing them they were in Ferreirola, and from a slightly elevated vantage point they could make out the vague outline of the footpath heading out across the moor land towards the village opposite, Busquistar, if I remember.

They walked for a further thirty minutes, trying to follow a path that didn't want to be followed. Dense woodland offered shade, while lemon, lime, orange and mango trees, untouched and growing wildly gave them pleasant distraction. They continued through it until the landscape opened up to reveal an old scorched threshing ground. Right in the middle of it they saw a shadowy figure dressed in black. The father put his arm across the boys protectively, and with more than a hint of over reaction he ordered them to stop. Surveying the situation from his new vocation of army general, he made his critical analysis. Man thrashing around with a sword making devastating cuts at thin air, bad sign and a possible threat to life.

He checked him once more, head still, moving only his eyes, noting the absolute swiftness and grace the enemy moved with. After a few moments he stopped his imaginary mass murder and lowered his sword, and with the threat lessoned the family were ordered to retreat, finding a suitable diversion around crazy sword man. It was José who recognised him as the man from Aljibe, prompting concerned father to repeat his advice to his sons and telling them once more to keep away.

Juan however felt drawn to the mysterious figure with the sword. Well he would, being Juan. He tried to analyse as to why he might feel this connection. Maybe it was the direct way in which he spoke to them the day before. Maybe it was a natural rebellion because his father had warned him off, or maybe it was something else.

They finally reached the village opposite, a sleepy sun scorched home for a tiny population of hardy inhabitants. It sat proudly on top of the hill with the obligatory church poking out, visible from all angles and the main advertiser in town, looming and almost threatening, important or irrelevant, depending only on your level of religious manipulation.

The heat of the day had introduced itself, the mountains in summer being a good few degrees hotter than the coast, forcing the four of them to look for a shop selling water for the return trip, badly regretting their oversight.

The journey back seemed much easier, what with the slope in their favour and the relief of hydration. They arrived back at the threshing ground and simultaneously remembered the man with the sword. Eight eyes scanned fervently before the four heads nodded in agreement that the coast was clear and walking could commence.

Back at the house they shared their opinions about the strange man with the sword, but only one of them was sufficiently intrigued enough to ponder a chance meeting.

12

GAIN ALL KNOWLEDGE

In the coming months and years you will need to be ahead of the game. Ignorance, apathy, and misplaced trust in your world leaders will cost you your life.

Later, that same afternoon, Juan, fuelled with curiosity, enthusiasm, and a little apprehension took another walk, leaving José and David watching nonsense television and dad, taking the siesta tradition very seriously.

He walked in the heat of the day, the sun was unforgiving and scorched him every time he popped out of the shade. His youthful ignorance paid it no respect, propelling him through the little streets of Methina, quickly finding himself, only partially intentionally, standing outside Aljibe. He weighed it up from the safety of fifteen metres, knowing he had to go in after craftily convincing himself he was suffering from dehydration. One last deep breath of normality before he entered the world of the unknown, patiently battling the annoying fly traps.

Once inside he focused only on the bar, eyes locked forward, too apprehensive to look around. His shrewd senses told him the restaurant was probably empty, and studying a rack full of crisps he contemplated his options. Before a plan B was formed he felt a presence directly behind him.

"Can I be of assistance to you?"

Juan turned around sharply, stifling his obvious shock, scrambling for plausible words.

"Oh, I didn't know you worked here," he mumbled, straightening imaginary creases from his shirt.

"I don't work anywhere," the man replied, equally shocked by Juan's lack of awareness. "I do however serve the people of this village with the things they think they need though, and throw in a few extras for good measure," he continued. "Now what do you think you need?"

Alfonso stood at just five feet six inches, perfectly proportioned and conservative with his movements, almost gliding his way around. His hair had a tinge of grey around the ears, the short black fringe adding a convincing youthfulness. Apart from the laughter lines around the eyes he had a complete lack of wrinkles, an unusual feature for a Mediterranean man.

"Just a glass of water please," Juan squeaked.

"Excellent choice," the man answered, nodding and grinning approval. "Do you know that drinking just eight glasses of this wonderful liquid daily and ingesting half a teaspoon of rock salt or sea salt can keep you in perfect health and cure almost every ailment from blood pressure problems to mental illness, and everything else in between? And if it comes pure from the mountains like this one, well even better."

"I didn't know that," Juan shyly remarked.

"I know you don't, so few do. And why do you think that is?"

Before Juan had chance to answer he jumped in the gap.

"It is because this simple knowledge is not presented to you. We have surgeons transplanting organs and doing other incredible feats of medicinal wizardry, yet they have never studied the effects of keeping the body hydrated with water, or even the effects of nutrition and the body. Strange when you think the body is made up of around 75% water and the brain around 85% water.

Did you know that the vast majority of the world is dying of dehydration? Yes I did say dying, every day. And the cure is in a glass of water, or a few glasses. No medication, no operation, no funeral. Of course the heads of the pharmaceutical companies may know it, but what do you think would happen to their corrupt money if the world could be kept healthy by drinking enough water daily? They have a vested interest in withholding this information."

"But why would doctors let people die?" Juan naively asked, a frown clearly visible on his young forehead.

"There are two reasons. Firstly, only a few doctors know the truth themselves, they are merely puppets in the hands of a much higher power. They blindly continue dispensing drugs or theories which only seek to serve the agenda of those in control. Vast amounts of money are made on a system that sees most in way too early graves. Even most of your politicians have no idea what the actual agenda is, they only see the level they work on. In fact, pharmaceutical companies can yield more power than governments. These people are wearing blinkers and looking forward to their next pay increase, or the bonus they will receive for being stupid. They are not necessarily bad, just a bit dim.

Now the second types are the ones who know the full story. These we could call evil, or maybe loveless would be a kinder expression. And yes, some of them are running our countries. So when people naively ask the question, "Why don't the government do something about this or about that?" when the solution is glaringly obvious, it is simply because they don't want to solve the problem. It is better for them to have society that is living in fear and frustration than a society who feel free, powerful and dynamic. They would be much harder to control wouldn't they?

For example, are you aware that cancer is being prevented and even cured by the use of a simple vitamin? Metabolic therapy is the name."

"No, I didn't know that," Juan said again, feeling a tall hat with the letter D emerging.

"Oh yes my friend," he said, laughing loudly, rocking back and forth on his heels.

Juan felt like his head was coming off, the world he thought he knew was being turned upside down by a rocking madman.

"The cure for cancer is known, the cure for cancer is known," he repeated, louder still.

"Have you ever heard of the old disease called scurvy?"

Again Juan had no time to answer.

"Yes scurvy the incurable, killed millions you know. Do you know what brought it to an end? Do you know what complex and fantastic cure was found? Vitamin C," he yelled, the announcement tipping him over the preacher's precipice, laughing with a complete absence of embarrassment before breaking out into a chorus of "Oranges and lemons said the bells of St Clements."

"That's it folks, oranges and lemons introduced into the diet, wiped out the incurable disease instantly.

It's exactly the same with cancer, different vitamin that's all, B17 your fellow this time, gone from our diet. Most modern diets have as much nutrition in them as a plate full of cardboard. The nutrients of B17 are stored as an enzyme, pancreatic to be precise. When cancer, which begins its journey as a cleansing process, gets to a certain point in its evolution, the enzyme is released and kills it at that stage. Scientifically proven I might add. Small traces of cyanide gas the deadly weapon there. Now if the enzyme is not present, it can't be released and the process is allowed to continue and ravage the cells.

Cancer is a metabolic disease and the cure is metabolic therapy. Special clinics all over the world are successfully treating cancer. Nutrition, nutrition, nutrition! I could also say to you it is a fungal disease and should be treated as a fungus," he said, cupping his mouth and whispering fungus into Juan's ear, driving the point home.

"Many cultures throughout the world have not had a single case of cancer in their history, not one. Guess what their diet had an abundance of? B17 of course. Combined with a healthy diet, organic of course, enough clean water, vitamin C, vitamin A, plenty of exercise and fresh air, this little secret should see you still enjoying life at 120. Keep your eye on your vitamin D intake too, the sunshine vitamin. Fortunately for us we have abundance of wonderful sunshine, but for those who don't, they need the supplement, and a lot of it too."

"I thought sunshine gave you cancer," Juan asked.

"Ha Ha, they got *you* with that one too did they? How can the sun give you cancer? You only need to stop and think. It has been here for a long time my friend. Maybe it's the ozone layer then. Maybe it is global warming which is of course is caused by the human being and his polluted lifestyle and has nothing to do with the activity of the sun and natural cyclical behaviour patterns. Yes it must be those C.O.2 emissions, our government scientists say so. Let me tell you Juan, they will cause more environmental damage cutting down the trees from the forest to make the paper for the "Climate tax" forms they are no doubt preparing."

"Why would they say those things then?" Juan said, trading fear and curiosity in micro seconds.

"Fear is a big one; keep everyone terrified and asking the government what they are going to do about it and they have instantly given all their power away. What are WE going to do about it would make much more sense.

Money, there's another thing. There are billions invested in the ignorance of climate change and it wouldn't do to stand in its way, if you know what I mean. Good scientists who are serious in their efforts to find the genuine cause of it are being discredited, struck off, ridiculed, and even killed."

"Killed?" Juan managed to shriek, outrage visible from head to foot.

"Oh did I say killed? I meant died in mysterious circumstances. It is important to step back from the hysteria of all propaganda and go to a quiet place inside of you and see how you feel about it. Let's go back to the sun for a moment. We have an increase in skin cancer, that's certain. We are ordered to buy and apply ever increasing amounts of sun cream from the "don't step outside without your cream, you might die" brigade. You would be better off researching what is in those sun creams. Now let me see, I just wonder if any of them could have carcinogenic ingredients. Most lotions filter out UVB while allowing in UVA, thus ensuring no vitamin D is made. UVA is the UV component which actually damages the skin, causing skin cancer. The incidents of skin cancer soared dramatically as the sun lotion campaign took hold. Now I am not suggesting that you can burn your skin without risk, not at all. But we need vitamin D to prevent cancer and the propaganda machine is determined to stop your exposure to the sun, even to the extent of military planes spraying chemicals and leaving huge trails across the sky which you can clearly see form a barrier between the sun and us."

Juan felt he was having all the mysteries of the world poured over his head, drowning yet trying to remember every word, not even knowing if he would ever meet this man again. He was concentrating so hard he was oblivious of everything around him, long since forgetting what he had come in for, reminded only by the verbal prompt.

"Don't forget your water."

"Thank you erm . . ."

"Alfonso is the name, it means noble and ready. And you are Juan?"

"Yes," he said, without thinking about how he might have known, without thinking about the water he was gulping down, without thinking about the skin at the side of his thumb he was frantically picking, without thinking about the depth of the hole he had just voluntarily dropped in.

Alfonso shook his hand very gently and looked deep into his eyes, deep enough to cause the usual uneasiness of a comfort zone entered, yet paradoxically bringing Juan reassurance.

"I'm glad you came to see me, it's saved us a lot of time. I am at your service whenever you can visit. Your father does not want you to come so be careful; he doesn't understand we are old friends."

Juan never responded. He merely offered his thanks and left.

Outside, the day was behaving as normal, sun dutifully shining, usual insect drone present, people attending to unimportant business, nothing to suggest to Juan that the world was any different at all.

The speed of his walk increased, rushing through the narrow cobbled streets, confusion and fear winning the battle of his senses.

He noticed nothing of his journey back, not the car which narrowly missed him, not the two dogs barking at each other in the street, not the old lady carrying too many bags in that heat. By the time he reached Los Monteros the heavy blanket of truth had lifted slightly and snippets of Alfonso's conversations were filtering through. He realised what he had said about being old friends and about saving time coming to Aljibe. He tried to think as to why he had said those things, he tried desperately, but logic had left town.

He entered the house and walked straight through to the back, sat down and looked towards the mountains, hoping somehow they were old enough and wise enough to help him. He hoped, wished, and prayed, but the big old beast remained tight lipped.

13

UNIFORMS

If everyone refused to wear a soldier's uniform there would surely be no more wars. Can you imagine the cowardly politicians fighting one themselves?

"Hey Jack, how will I fit all the wisdom and knowledge I have here into that tiny earth body?" Annie asked him, regal like, with an air of self mocking snootiness.

"Take what you can and come back for the rest later," he laughed.

"You make it sound so easy Jack," she replied, knowing as she did that it would not be long before she joined Joseph once more. The plan was unfolding, vibrations were changing and in her own way, unnoticeably she hoped, she began to detach a little from her friends, a self protecting kind of preparation.

"Of course it is easy, you are not learning anything you don't already know, just remembering that you are all knowing. Yes you will get caught in that three dimensional prison and never see the bars, and what seems like an easy choice between being a small, scared, and restricted human trapped in a shell, and breaking the shell to become the multi dimensional genius capable of manifesting the great love and abundance you are, will not be so easy when you are there. You will get worn down with the speed of life, the pressure of survival and mundane tick tock we call living.

Week after week, month after month and year after year of this existence leaves people disconnected from their purpose. They get bored with their lives and their lives become boring. They have no quality there and they can't find the inspiration to change it. That's why we get nudged back on track, or our world turned upside down if we don't respond to the nudges. Then, in those darkest moments we are inspired to look deeper at the meaning of our existence.

Hopefully we realise the universe is never wrong and is just giving us what we need. It never makes mistakes. Maybe we never fully appreciate the fact that if the universe stopped thinking about us for one second, we would exist no more. It takes only a minute of correct thinking however to realise how lucky the human is, how lucky the bird that flies free, the trees and the flowers that grow, lucky because the universe has chosen to express itself through all these different mediums.

In fact everything we do is expressing a part of that infinity. It's unbelievable that we are given such a gift and do not appreciate it. We should try to express ourselves in the most unique and original way, that's the least we can do."

"Yes, I agree. And I will try. I just hope I don't disappoint."

"The thing is we are all going from dark to light, from fear to trust and from limitation to abundance. It's the purpose of our existence. You can't really disappoint Annie; we will all arrive there eventually, no matter how long it takes. For me, I prefer to hurry up," he said, jogging on the spot for emphasis.

"Just think, by the time I meet Joseph he will already have lived eighteen earth years, and yet, strangely, it's as if he has only just left."

"Yes I know. It is strange, this time thing for sure," Florence said, a tokenistic offering to allow her into the conversation.

"It follows such a defined structure on Earth. Seconds, minutes, hours, days, weeks, months, years and so on. It is almost impossible to break its relentless pattern. We get influenced, no programmed, that's the word, programmed to believe time is real. We are born, we age and we die. But what if we refused this programme? What if we rewrote it somehow? What if our infinite consciousness could override the programme and rewrite the messages to our brain? Imagine never aging, or at least slowing it right down because it's deleted from our programme, past, present and future all happening at the same time, and time, demoted to nothing more than the illusion it is. The lunatics in the loop escaping. Do you think its possible Annie?" she added, with childlike enthusiasm.

"I promise I'll certainly try when I get there Florence. I may lose a few illusory years of my life when they lock me away for my beliefs though. It's difficult to hold a point of view which is diametrically opposed to everyone else's, you know that."

"It shouldn't stop us from believing it though," Florence encouraged, her tone changing from advisory to almost a demanding one.

"No you're right. I think it's a great contributory factor to the state the Planet Earth is in. When you feel something different but conform to what everyone else sees as normal, it's like, well it's dishonest really. And it has become so severe it's allowed the world to be continually run by evil people.

I know ninety five percent of the population, if not more, don't want any war, or poverty, or nuclear energy, or starving countries, but the dishonesty in them makes them ignore it. We could call it apathy also but I feel it's stronger than that.

Just imagine that, ninety five percent wanting love and peace, yet allowing a tiny five percent to run the show. Why do they do it? Why don't they wake up and see where the power lies? And the maddest part of all is the fact that all it needs is the word no. No violence necessary, no fighting back, no riots, just a collective no. How could they then impose their extortionate interest rates on a world that refuses to pay it? How could they ensure that nations die of starvation if other countries made sure everything was distributed fairly? And how could they create wars for profit if everyone refuses to put on a soldiers uniform? They would hardly fight it themselves would they? What could a few thousand do with over six billion souls saying no thanks? The world needs people to stop turning the other cheek. It needs people to start thinking about the survival of their beautiful planet and not just how things affect them personally. It really is time to do it before it's too late. If everyone collectively does this, an inner healing of the world will surely take place. Just this shift of consciousness would mean Mother Earth would not have to heal herself by bringing tremendous turmoil to the planet. Isn't that how it works?"

They talked this way for a long time before Annie announced she wanted to be alone. She could feel the time arriving for her journey. She hugged her friends with conviction, urgency in her words.

"I will be leaving very soon, love you to the world and back," she said, passion and intensity driving the words home.

"Take care of each other you two; we will be together again soon, you know that."

"Without a doubt," Jack said with cock sure confidence. "Joseph will be holding you in his arms before long. Go and enjoy your time together, tell him not to worry about anything, he'll soon be home."

"Goodbye Jack, goodbye Florence."

She faded out of sight and Jack and Florence were left clutching at the cosmos.

"Let her go Jack," Florence softly said. "She needs to be alone now; waiting is always the hardest thing."

The wait wasn't a long one, swirling spirals, bright lights and vivid colours were followed by the magnetic pull towards her future. Annie's infinite consciousness would soon be sitting in the cockpit of her new vehicle, and that vehicle will be sitting in the infinite consciousness of Joseph. Job done.

14

NEWS

You will find it almost impossible for good news to be reported, no matter how far you travel. Bad news however will find you wherever you are. So if something good happens to you, tell everyone you meet. If not make something up. When they say isn't it awful about the hurricane damage, tell them it blew a bunch of money through your window. If they can lie about everything being awful, so can you.

It was a long hot summer's day with a humid evening attached to it the night Annabelle and Eammon broke the news.

They had met the previous summer at a music event on the glorious Achille Island, where Annabelle and two of her friends had gone to watch Irish folk bands perform. Eammon, very much on his own territory, living only a stone throw from the pub, was there to watch his friend, a talented, rubber armed drummer who was playing in one of the bands. He sat alone while his friend and the other band members went through their collection of local tales set to infectious rhythms and up tempo beats.

The girls arrived later, like girls do, halfway through the set in fact, nosily setting up camp on his table. By the time the band had finished their set, Eammon and Annabelle were locked in a world inaccessible to all outsiders.

The evening of music came and went, but the destiny of new love waved a flag that said permanent. Over the course of that summer they became inseparable, Eammon making the journey from Pacific Drive on Achille Island to Mulranny on a daily basis. It wasn't a difficult thing to do mind, the drive was a breathtaking journey in itself, combining the rolling hills of County Mayo and the beautiful ocean and spectacular views of Achille Island.

A more satisfying drive would have been difficult to find. Eammon however would have done it regardless, distance being no match for the expedition of romance, besides which, he had been made more than welcome in the O Malley home, Roy and Margaret thought very highly of him they did, and that thought was effortlessly reciprocated.

A builder by trade, Eammon had applied his skills to various parts of Annabelle's house. He did this with a genuine enthusiasm, enjoying transforming their modest home and coyly accepting the obvious accolade that followed. His efforts were appreciated by Annabelle's mother and father who were grateful for his kindness, not only to Annabelle but to themselves also. They looked forward to their nights in together and the infectious optimism new love brings to a household.

This particular evening, the evening of confessions, they had all walked down to the beach at Mulranny. Margaret, carefully placed between two great rocks, which acted as a windbreak, watched Eammon chasing Annabelle along the beach and then a quick reversal of roles as Annabelle showed her love by wrestling him to the floor and punching his arms.

Roy was busy too, collecting shells for the lid of a small jewellery box he was making. He was in his element here, searching through the whirlpools for the treasures they harboured. He had spent many years of his life walking these parts and knew every twist and turn. It was his home and he had never desired to travel.

"Come on you two," Margaret shouted to the oblivion of new love. Roy gave them a signal and they ran over to where Margaret was sitting. Annabelle gave her a hug and they set off across grass and sand, homewards through the heather. Five minutes, that's all it was, before they were back on the road that led to their house. Eammon pushed Margaret's wheelchair and dad and daughter lagged a little behind.

They arrived at the house and the kettle was on before their coats were off, Roy the kettle king in superb form.

Annabelle's nonchalance faltered as shallow breathing and sweaty palms set out their awkward stall. She wondered how her mum would feel about the fact they were so young. She had no worries about her dad, he was not known for over reacting. Anyway, this is how it happened, I remember it well.

"Mum, Dad, we have something to tell you," she finally announced, Eammon standing next to her, holding her with one arm firmly around her shoulder, defending her from an attack which never came.

"Me and Eammon are going to have a baby."

The words were rushed but the response delayed. She looked up at her father who was already beaming one of his huge grins. "One down," she thought to herself.

"Hee Hee, that's great news," he laughed.

She bit hard on her bottom lip and looked across to her mum who now wanted to know where they would live, how they would manage, if they would get married and what the child would be named.

"Let's enjoy this night and we can leave the rest till later," Roy said, intentionally infectiously. "We are going to be grandparents Margaret, so many great times ahead."

And with that brief summary he went to the cabinet with the cracked pain, took out four glasses for the wine, ignoring the boiled water in the kettle.

15

ART

Forget teaching the maths, the science, the history and the physics. Walk all children through the world of music, art and dance and watch their true genius in all subjects unfold.

Juan didn't get chance to see Alfonso for another two days. However a sweltering start to the day provided a fraction sized glimmer of hope, and the reluctance to leave the coolness of the house from his dad and brothers was seized upon by Juan the opportunist.

"I think I'll take a walk," he said unexcitedly, hoping his apathetic tone ensured no-one would be joining him. The response was fortunately pathetic and he left without another word.

Juan had thought of nothing but Alfonso the mystery man, who seemed to know so much about him and everything else in the world. He hadn't slept properly since the meeting at Aljibe, and he had been told to stop daydreaming more than once.

He took the footpath once more to Ferreirola, following its twisted trajectory until he came out at the old threshing ground, the place where he had seen Alfonso cutting invisible men with his sword.

Surveying the area he saw nothing more than a few rocks and bushes, scorched on burnt earth, brutally punished for ten months a year without a hope of shade.

He sat down on a large rock and tried to neutralise any preconceptions of his predicament. A jumbo jet whistled far off. He followed its noise until his eyes located it, leaving its trail of silver behind.

"When you begin painting you must not have any artist or style in your mind. You must keep your mind free of all influence. Your brush must also be without mind. Paint what you feel inside, your eyes alone cannot be trusted. It's not your eyes you see with."

Alfonso was standing right behind him, how he got there unnoticed would be only one of the mysteries he was about to reluctantly own.

"What does this mean; you don't see with your eyes?" Alfonso asked, more of himself than of Juan. "The purpose of the eyes is only to change what you look at into electrical signals. The brain then interprets this into a three dimensional reality. The eyes are only receptors, sending the signals to the brain which then decodes the signals into all you see and believe to be real. Without the brain there is no picture. Only waves of energy. Waves of energy young man and that's it!

When people say it's all in your mind it's almost true. The world and the universe are all in your brain. What great news! You can create whatever you desire. But be careful also, your reality can be created for you by others. Brainwashing they call it. So do not let your eyes restrict or deceive you. And remember one more thing. You can never paint something wrong, there are no rules. Rules are spiritual handcuffs for fools. Good morning," he laughed.

"Good morning," Juan replied, shaking his head with bemusement.

"Begin your quest while you are hungry. It will be much easier like that. Your natural talent will create the opportunity, your persistence and beliefs will carry you wherever you choose to go. You do not have to give up your music either. Both arts will allow you to communicate your message. It is a privilege to perform an art."

Juan hadn't noticed the sword at his side until he picked it up suddenly and began slicing at thin air again, first one direction then another. Every cut produced a whooshing sound with the sheer power created. He moved with such speed Juan struggled to focus on the action being displayed. He finished his sequence with two full spins, then triumphantly poked the sword to the heavens before bringing it back down, very slowly, and extending it forwards from his chest area. He remained in this pose for a full five minutes. Not one movement, not one blink of an eye, not a word uttered. Juan was transfixed, blinking profusely.

"Action in stillness and stillness in action," he eventually said. "So much life in what appears to have no movement. Don't make the

Now bring yourself back to your surroundings, back to your body. Become aware of your whole self. Now open your eyes."

Juan tried but had to shut them immediately, the brightness of the sun uncompromising. When he finally adjusted them, the first thing he saw was Alfonso standing ram-rod straight.

"Posture and alignment is the key to expansion," he chortled. "Of all the children I see and most of the adults too, I rarely see one with good posture. Every time you slouch or drop your head and stoop, you are cutting off your connection with the universe. How serious is that? When your spine is straight and your head is held up, you are, what I would call, aligned. With this posture you can connect with those universal energies, they can travel down and through you like a conduit. Likewise, the Earth energies are coming up through your feet and legs, the very same energies that facilitate the growth of all the flowers and trees, even the food which sustains you. You might say you are the connection between heaven and Earth. Now do you see the power in that?"

Juan stretched up as far as he could, embarrassed by his crumpled body. He wondered if Alfonso had finished with today's lecture, before he swung around to impart some more wisdom on him.

"On a more tangible level, consider your internal organs. When you slouch in your arm chair and slump forward, your torso becomes constricted and all your internal organs are literally crushed. Think about your digestive system struggling in that tiny space. Then there is your liver and your lungs and kidneys. Due to a combination of bad posture and incorrect breathing you are only using a third of your lungs capacity when you breathe. With practice it is possible to use the whole of the lung whilst breathing. With practice it is possible to take one breath per minute, imagine what a difference this would make to your life. We know breathing is important. If we don't do it we die. But it can be so much more. It is the elixir of life.

When you inhale you are bringing in fresh healing energy. When you focus on this aspect it becomes very powerful. As you exhale you are releasing toxins from your body and also negative energy. The very thing that keeps you alive is given no thought whatsoever by most people. Stretch up Juan, even more! Now you see you have doubled the space in there, maybe trebled. Your organs are thanking you for making their lives more comfortable, they are working more efficiently already. Your energy will circulate so much better. Don't they show you these things at school?" he laughed.

"They don't show us anything of interest," Juan remarked. Not sure whether he would be in trouble for his seemingly disrespectful analysis of authority.

"What do you think of your teachers?" Alfonso asked him casually.

"Some are nice and some are not. It's not so much what they are like though, it's more that I get so bored with what they teach me."

Juan felt pleased with this answer, his longest one yet.

"I don't even believe half of what they saying," he added, growing in confidence.

"Your scepticism is correct young man. But they are teaching you only what they know. If they knew the full story most of them would want to share it with you, but unfortunately it's hit and miss history, sci-fi science, and very fishy physics. However, if a teacher is enlightened and tries to teach children the deeper aspects of life, they will very quickly be made to tow the lying line. The curriculum is rigorously regimented, fiercely guarded and ruthlessly geared towards your left brain. If the right brain isn't stimulated you will become bored very easily. The right brain is to do more with the art and all creative issues. The left brain is more to do with logic and if you always look for logic you will always miss the magic. Your comically named education system is nothing more than a method to trap people in the left side of their brain, making them prisoners of logic, time, structure and forcing them to accept, and indeed create a reality of human life that is a fraction of what it could be. Every aspect of the society you live in has been crudely created by the intellect. Schools, colleges and universities adore an intellectual that will score well in the examinations set by all the other intellectuals running our lives."

He stopped briefly, closed his eyes and covered his forehead with his right hand, a gesture Juan interpreted to mean that the very thought of all these facts pained Alfonso greatly.

"Let me ask you a question Juan," he said softly. "Where is the consciousness and the love, the heart and the compassion in the education system? Are they turning out creative, multi-dimensional, loving genius incarnate, or a society of robots hoping to be a bigger cog than their fellow pupils? When you stimulate only the left brain it keeps you from expanding your awareness to all the different dimensions you are capable of perceiving. It locks you into a certain frequency. Please accept my crude analogy but it does remind me somewhat of a computer. You can do many brilliant things on there such as designing, organising and storing information etc. Now, stimulating the right hemisphere of the brain is like logging your computer onto the internet where you can open up to a huge dimension of information. Being on the internet gives you the freedom to access any dimension you have an interest in. You may study hypnosis, or read about alternative healing, martial arts or travel, anything and everything you feel like. Once you log off however it's back to logic, reason and limitation. Your consciousness is the internet and your current state of mind is just Microsoft Word. Your consciousness is also under constant bombardment. Understand what I am about to say and you will benefit more than I could ever tell you."

Juan knew he was serious in his statement. He had that concerned look Juan had begun to recognise.

"Take it as true that there are forces out there who wish to suppress your true nature. More than this, they do not care if you live or die. They have an agenda which wishes to control every single person on the planet, even to the point of micro chipping every man, woman and child, carried forward under the false threat of national security, or quite possibly a mass vaccination programme through a fabricated virus. Technology has seen the development of a micro chip that can fit inside a needle. They call it Nano technology. Once you have the chip in your body your days of freedom are over. It is all in place."

Juan looked uncomfortable with this latest announcement and Alfonso realised he may have gone too far, too soon.

"Do not worry Juan, the end is not written yet. You are in the middle of the story. You have the opportunity with over six billion others to write it how you wish. It is truly the most remarkable time this Earth has ever known. We are in the middle of a huge transformation and it is a real opportunity for mankind."

Juan took a big breath, the tightened chest forcing the exaggerated gasp.

"Why would a microchip be the end of our freedom?"

"Like I said, the technology is already in place. It is already old news. Trust what I am saying. From a central bank they will be able to send signals both individually and on mass to the chips in the bodies of every person on the planet. Facts, facts, facts," he reiterated.

"They can control your emotions, your thoughts, make you ill, make you murder, and even kill you at random, individually or on mass. It is the jewel in their crown to total control. Check out what I am saying Juan. It is all there to see. You have been blessed with the internet. You do not need to be in the dark. They rely only on the fact that you won't do the research, or when you discover the plan, that you feel so powerless you will feel too insignificant or even too embarrassed to tell anyone else.

If there is only one thing you take away from me Juan, please let it be this. The awakening of the world's consciousness is the main purpose of your incarnation."

Alfonso adjusted his posture; Juan read the signal that it would be a long lecture and tried to stretch up. He wondered if this would ever come naturally.

"Who are these people?"

"They are different to you and me. Just know that. They are different. Your consciousness has been kidnapped. You and millions of others are operating on a fraction of your capability. These forces are controlling every single aspect of your life. I know it is hard to understand this as you think you have free will to do as you please.

And you do have free will, but free will for most is only to choose one reality they control over another one they control. Whether you're waving a flag that says "Ban the bomb" or a flag that says "Bomb the bad," you are still waving a flag with a flag wavers mentality. You are still fighting for a cause. They know that a fighting mentality is no threat to them. The only threat is when you are coming from the aspect of unconditional love, this they have no defence for. Left wing fights with right wing while they drive their plans straight through the centre.

Look what happens to people who know the answer is love and dare to speak it. John Lennon, Martin Luther King, Bill Hicks, Bob Marley, Diana Spencer, Michael Jackson and so many more, all removed one way or another before their time. Of course Bob Marley and Michael Jackson died of illness's. Didn't they?

They control the day to day theatre of life in which you function and in which you think you have freedom, but you are only being allowed to see a tiny aspect of what is possible.

They allow and even instigate all wars and conflicts which lock society into a survival mode. This serves as a double bonus as while we are fighting amongst ourselves, we are taking our eye off the main problem, the leaders and the basic freedoms they are removing.

You see Juan, when we are focused on our survival we become completely fearful. When we live in fear we always give our power away to the people who are controlling our fear. It is a vicious circle, more vicious than you will know.

Why do you think it is that no matter how hard you work you are always just above the poverty line? You are totally absorbed in paying your way, hanging on to your home, feeding your family etc. You have no time or energy to expand your awareness and see your existence for what it is. Once you know you are infinite consciousness in a physical body, and that you can never die or cease to exist then you are free. The minute you realise this they lose the power over you. You are not dependent upon those powers to keep you alive because you know death is not possible. Only life and change is possible. And there is the key to understanding your whole existence. The secret is to lose your fear of survival because you know death does not exist. You can never die Juan. That's it! You can never die."

With that Alfonso began laughing uncontrollably. He gained control this time, shortly after he lost it.

"You just move to another place of your choice. Part of you can also be here too. You will be able to stay with the people you like to be around. You are multi dimensional; you never have to leave the people you love. Think about those feelings of love you have for your family and friends. How can that not continue? No one ever leaves Juan. You are surrounded by the so called dead; they are right next to you, living the same as you. You will return to this planet many times, choosing the people you love, to act out various roles which enable you all to grow. You have to learn many things Juan, compassion, forgiveness, unconditional love, self empowerment and a hundred other virtues, until you have evolved into the all knowing spirit we all eventually become. You have spirit guides to assist and direct you too. Why would you fear death when you know this truth? Try it now, ask your guides for direction. Ask them to support you in your artwork, or anything else you like. There is no great trick to this. You don't have to sit on top of a mountain quoting scriptures. How many scriptures you can remember and recite will be of no use to you. It's more to do with how many obstructions you can remove. Sit quietly for a moment, take a minute to settle your mind, and find a quiet place. Now, just ask the question you want answering, ask for that guidance."

Juan sat quiet and began to invite those spirit guides to help him with his dream of becoming an artist. He didn't see anyone in his mind, but he did feel as though someone or something might be there.

"Please help me to become an artist," Juan said in his mind.

"Juan," Alfonso whispered. "Try it again, but this time use the words like this."

Juan kept his eyes shut and his ears open.

"Now I am a successful artist, allow my work to impact and influence people for their highest spiritual growth."

Alfonso said it stretching the words out to amazing lengths.

"The way you use the words is important. Intent is an incredibly powerful action we have all but forgotten about"

Juan repeated the phrase word for word; all background noise seemed to fade away, holding him in his bubble of bewilderment. He stayed with this emptiness and tried to imagine what his spirit guide might look like. He felt his heart opening up and a kind of light pouring in there.

Alfonso's acute guidance, in short, would be the shortcut Juan desired, a hands on development of his raw energy.

16

ASKING

If you didn't know where you were going you would surely ask for directions. So if you're not sure which path to take in life, why not throw a question to the stars? Unless you're certain we humans are the only life in a universe with no end, it maybe worth a shot.

Soran was in deep discussion with Jack and Florence, putting the universe to rights when his clairvoyant cloak was firmly tugged.

"Delmore is communicating," he announced excitedly, cutting dead the holographic conversation.

"Great news, you always said he would one day," Jack said encouragingly.

Soran focused in on the energy of Delmore, matching the resonance of his vibration to bring about the information he needed. He saw what he had to do and how to guide him to the opportunities available. The path was there and he just needed Delmore to read the signs. That's all.

"It is enough Juan," Alfonso said, jolting him back to a field in Las Alpujarras. "Try to be creative with your interpretation of the signs, being aware is also one the most beneficial qualities you can possess. Tomorrow you may fall and break a leg and wonder how that could possibly be a sign you were being helped by guides and spirits. Then the day after, when there is nothing else to do but sit with your leg sticking up, you begin to paint your mountain. And by the next day you have produced a masterpiece which sets you off on a lifelong love affair with painting, a feat you may never have achieved without those prevalent circumstances."

Alfonso caught a glimpse of Juan's face, the look of terror there being sufficient for him to inject the life saving sound of laughter.

"Don't worry Juan," he said through another raucous bout of it. "I didn't mean you were going to break your leg. This crazy old fool doesn't know everything, I am merely giving examples."

"I knew that," Juan lied.

"Of course you did, know this also. You cannot get through this life unscathed, you come from the source and you will return there someday. The experiences you take back will be your treasures. When things seem terrible, or you are beside yourself with problems and worries, remember you are capturing a huge experience to take back with you. Don't get caught up too much in this reality. It is not permanent, just a temporary illusion. This is not your home. You will not get through this incarnation without your battle scars. They will be emotional and physical ones. Own them and be grateful for the rich stories you can take back and re tell to your friends. Don't go back and bore them to death, think of your problems and how you work with them as wonderful little stories. Get your teeth into the big ones and if they keep getting repeated, be sure you have come to master those. Deal with them one at a time as they arise, then let go."

Alfonso checked on Juan, reading his expression carefully before saying this. "Normally when people have problems they tend to internalise them, which means they keep them in their head and go over them time and time again. They become dark inside. They become heavy too. There is nowhere for the problem to go because the only place they believe in is in the head. Now then," Alfonso said, tapping his index finger on the side of his left temple. "I have some groundbreaking news, a real live hot off the press shocker. You have a place just below your navel, this place has many names but it doesn't need any. When you have a problem, an idea, or even just an ambitious thought, try to breathe it into this centre. Close your eyes and concentrate on it going in there, and then out to infinity. Let the universe deal with it, it's big enough. You can put all your problems in this place and allow them to be recycled there. If you really need a name you could call it your recycling centre. Let all be transformed into a positive outcome.

What would happen Juan, if you left all your rubbish out without it being recycled? Well your thoughts are the same," he answered, long before Juan could. "Years and years of wrong thinking, negativity, anger and anxiety, festering away with no way of release. It's a very smelly situation in there, very smelly. Here's another way of keeping light. If you can love things without condition it changes the reality of the situation. You have to love everything in your world and accept that it is perfect and progressing as it should. That is not to say you have to agree with all the wrongdoing of the world, far from it, just accept it and do your thing regardless. Loving unconditionally will correct society of many its problems."

The sun seemed to be sending a sign of agreement by turning up its intensity. Alfonso was also turning up the heat.

"As I said before, you are being constantly bombarded and suppressed in many different ways. They are targeting your food with chemicals such as aspartame (or amino sweet as it's cleverly named) and monosodium glutamate (M.S.G.) both of which have severe neurological effects and I recommend you avoid them at all costs. The introduction of genetically modified food, which will be the only food available if they get their way, is designed to genetically modify your D.N.A. This is all part of a little project is called "Codex Alimentarius." Again it is all verifiable facts; it is no secret or mere theory.

They shoot numerous vaccines into babies, over twenty in the first two years of that poor tiny body's life, which overloads and destroys the immune system, making sure every human is reliant upon the corruption of the pharmaceutical industry from birth to its premature death. Just look up some of the toxic chemicals they contain Juan. In fact, let me do it for you."

He looked up to the sky, took a deep breath and closed his eyes before narrating his long list.

"Aluminium hydroxide, Aluminium phosphate, Ammonium sulphate, animal tissues, pig blood, horse blood, rabbit brain, washed sheep red blood, dog kidney, monkey kidney, formaldehyde, mercury, phenoxyethanol, or anti freeze as it's better known, calf serum or bovine and Vero cells, a continuous line of monkey kidney cells. And that is only half of the toxic cocktail they claim to be essential to our health. Oh, and just the one small side effect of cancer, but nothing to worry about."

Juan was aghast with his ability to remember so many details and distressed with the content of what he had remembered. He wanted to question Alfonso but there was no pause in the outpouring just yet.

"They are putting fluoride in your water systems too, under the guise of protecting children's teeth. Can you imagine the same consciousness which indiscriminately carpet bombs countries, killing millions of innocent people for power and greed being so concerned with our children's cavities, that they would go to all that trouble and expense? I think not. Fluoride is a suppressor of the senses and makes you subservient."

He finished momentarily and allowed his guest a question.

"Where can I go to learn all these other things?" Juan asked inquisitively.

"To the mountains of course, there is a strange old man there who waves a stick and talks in riddles. Seriously, nobody can teach you anything Juan, they cannot tell you a truth. Truth has to be realised by you and you only. I can suggest things which may remind you of what you already know but have forgotten. Now then, if you prefer you can always go to school for eleven years and immerse yourself in the education system there, but it may take another eleven to unlearn all you have learned. Better to stay away in the first place. Do not listen to mainstream news. Do not read any newspaper and take it seriously. Do your research and find your truth. The whole planet has been duped and it breaks my heart to see what they have done to mankind."

Alfonso's voice trembled slightly, confirmation of his sadness to the hyper-sensitive Juan.

"You are here for a specific reason, it is your choice and despite this madness there has never been a better time to be alive. We are heading for massive change and tapping into the essence of existence and its true meaning. A wonderful creativity is bubbling. We are in the midst of a new- clear war on deceit, and truth will be the fuel to fire the rockets of revolution. The bombardment may be huge but the moment you laugh with understanding you will be free."

Alfonso put his arm around Juan with the heart felt compassion of a father to a son. Juan felt a little lighter, reassured, and not so alone.

"Today we have talked a lot. I have shown you that your world is not the one you knew. Please don't be afraid my good friend, it's better to come out of the dream and into truth. We will all arrive here eventually. In a few days time it will feel easier for you. You have your guides with you always, you are never alone. The spaces between you and me are oozing with life."

Juan felt as though he was giving him a farewell speech.

"Will I not see you again Alfonso," he sadly asked.

"Yes of course, we will meet here again in two days time. That will be the last time for a while. You have to go back to your village soon with all these new ideas. Remember though, you have learned what must seem like many complicated and grand theories, but in practice it is so simple. Keep your connection with the universe, love unconditionally and remember you are genius incarnate. That's it, keep it simple. Go back home and be the new village idiot."

Juan managed to laugh despite feeling smothered by the initial terror of truth. He had also lost all concept of time and asked Alfonso in a panic.

"We have only been here one hour. I am aware of your predicament and you will not be questioned on your return. Now see if you can run home without stopping, the physical exercise will ease your busy mind. Go now, I will see you soon enough."

"Thank you," was all Juan could manage, before setting off on a sprint. As he ran he tried to make sense of it all, the holiday, Alfonso, his future in this troubled world. He tried to run faster than his thoughts and as he pounded the ground beneath him, it served as a reminder that he was indeed still bound to this Earth, despite the feeling that his head was in the stars. A few breathless minutes later saw him outside Aljibe. As he looked towards the door he saw Alfonso waving and smiling at him.

He was about to stop and ask him how he had possibly gotten there so quickly when he remembered something he had said to him earlier.

"When you look with logic you miss the magic."

Pleased with his restraint and application of new found wisdom, he waved back at Alfonso and then ran by, onward to Los Monteros.

"Did you enjoy your walk?" his dad asked on his return, tone devoid of any suspicion.

"Yes thank you, I went across to the threshing ground and back."

"No strange man with the stick then?"

"No, I didn't see anyone," he lied.

"Let's eat something, you must be starving. Your brothers have gone to the shop for bread; we can make some sandwiches when they return."

Juan looked at his dad with a gratefulness he had previously lacked. He saw the kindness, gentleness and unswerving love he had always displayed for him, regardless of reciprocity. An unrivalled feeling of appreciation grew from deep within, galvanized by the depth of his conversation with the mountain wizard. He smiled a smile of genuine warmth for him.

When the brothers returned soon after, they prepared their food and took it through to the terrace. The mountain, unmoved by the events of Juan's day, offered him strength in silence. Juan felt he knew it just a little more this afternoon. He noticed its magnanimous stature, how it was grounded and routed to the Earth, yet somehow connected with the heavens also, all knowing; accepting whatever nature threw at it without judgement. It reminded him momentarily of his new friend.

He munched on his sandwich between thoughts. It tasted wonderful and he breathed in that pure mountain air, thinking to himself how life still held a glimmer of hope for him.

17

HOME

You can shut the door on this challenging world at night and hide in the created comfort of your home. Just don't forget who will be knocking first thing in the morning.

Annabelle and Eammon were timorously preparing for the birth of their first child. Kind donations had eased the financial side of things and more importantly cemented friendships and pruned the edges of the family tree.

There had started to rent a wonderful cottage close by, a stroke of luck, or simple synchronicity (depending on your viewpoint) had presented an opportunity they couldn't refuse.

The opportunity had arisen via Eammon's work. The repair and restoration of the old roof of the cottage had witnessed the necessary

connection with the owners, constructed over cups of tea and wonderful cakes.

The owner wanted the jobs completing on the house as quick as Eammon could manage, and Eammon could manage, a proper grafter, I think would be the term you use. The reason for the rush being that he and his wife were going to live in Kuwait for the next three years, his work in the oil industry had taken them to many parts of the globe already and Kuwait, well, just another pin to stick in his world atlas.

Eammon, the player of the crafty card had offered to look after and maintain the cottage while they were away. His hard work and diligence had already impressed the owner enough to trust him with this task. A small rental was agreed on and he had rushed home to share his great news with Annabelle and her folks.

The cottage was just a five minute walk from Roy and Margaret's house and Annabelle was naturally ecstatic with their quirky new home, enthusiastically putting her stamp on the cottage and fervently visualising their baby in there.

Roy could not believe his daughter was actually living in this cottage, this same cottage he had walked past a thousand times before, from being a small boy himself. He told them how he wished as a child that he could have lived in there; its storybook looks had fired his imagination every time he walked past. The closest he came being just a brief chat with the owner over the fence. Now he was coming to terms with the fact that he would be spending huge chunks of time there in his new role as Grandad. He laughed to himself at the mere thought of it all, the simplicity of life unfolding without any trace of struggle. He always knew in his heart that happiness costs nothing, and this latest episode in his life had also come absolutely free.

18

CHANGE

The mind loves everything to stay the same, that's the way it controls you. When you run naked through the bingo hall, it panics. So go on, show it who is boss.

Change was pressing its inevitability upon the peaceful, embryonic existence of Annie. She needed a heroic leap of faith to exit the cosy cocoon that had been home for the last few months. The pressure to expand into the unknown had finally become greater than the desire to remain in the familiar.

The cottage was ready and waiting for this very moment. The baby room was finished and the atmosphere was weighted with the powerlessness of the wait.

Annabelle had checked, re checked, and ticked her check list numerous times as the two of them stood in that nursery room, armed only with their collective urgency and intense imagination to visualise their baby in that Moses basket. But reality can be merciless at times and no amount of imagining would interfere with nature and its plans.

19

OWNERSHIP

When you register a child and receive a birth certificate, the child is then literally owned by the state. Every law can then be forced upon it. If you don't register the child, the state cannot take your child from you, no matter what the circumstances, as it does not belong to it. Interesting implications.

It was a cloudy evening with the constant threat of rain on the night of Annie's arrival. They had been trying to gauge the weather for an hour or so with regard to taking their usual evening walk, the clouds mocking their ability to analyse them by charging one way across the sky, then the other.

"Lets go anyway; we can take our waterproofs with us just in case," Annabelle eventually said, eight months, two weeks and two days into her pregnancy.

They headed off, Eammon with the backpack and Annabelle with her own load, down to the beach, with many little breaks; makeshift seats being formed from anything with a flattish surface, the last of these stops being a flat rock near a giant whirlpool. Under normal circumstances Annabelle and Eammon would have stayed there a while, contemplating their young lives, always with absolute optimism about their future together. Time usually lost some of its linear insistence in these moments, as conversation rolled, clipping corners and fraying the edges of reality. Not this night though, this night would be different.

"Let's head back now," Annabelle said after only a handful of minutes, leaving Eammon's face turning from one of relaxed smiles to frowns of concern. "Don't worry darling," she reassured him. "I'm alright." But she knew deep down, this would be the last time for many years they would undertake the walk as just a couple.

Halfway back they abandoned walking, and Eammon, in pure panic now, had to knock on the door of a friend, asking him with over animation to bring his car for Annabelle.

Back at the cottage the midwife was contacted and a long, life changing evening hung perilously over an anxious couple.

Eammon collected Margaret who wanted to be present at the birth. Roy said he'd prefer to stay at home and await news of his daughter and new Grandchild. Secretly he couldn't bear the thought of his beloved daughter in all that pain. He admired his wife's courage for having the strength to do it but knew he would be better off wearing his own carpet out with his continuous pacing.

The stubborn hours of the early morning, effortlessly elongated and refusing to co-operate with the desperate desires of Annabelle and Eammon were finally defeated. And just as dawn broke over the sea of Mulranny, the yell of new life rang through the cottage. A tiny expression of the universe was coming to terms with its fate, new beginnings with all memories erased and a blank canvas with which to paint her journey through another life upon.

The first label she acquired was her name. They called her Colleen and the birth certificate would soon collect the necessary data.

Annabelle gazed lovingly down at her old friend with no concept of the agreement the two of them made some eighteen Earth years ago. Joseph and Annie, mission accomplished.

Eammon telephoned Roy and relieved him of his worry.

"Hello Granddad," he began, with those same words almost every new parent breaks the news to their mum and dad with. "You have a beautiful Granddaughter," he told him excitedly.

Roy was predictably ecstatic as the world's weight lifted from his shoulders; the ensuing euphoria drove him straight to the kettle.

Another phone call to Pacific drive on Achille Island caused more screaming as another set of parents became Grand. And while all this was going on, Colleen's consciousness was drifting between the two worlds, floating out in the universe and then crashing back to the

Earth realm. It would be like this for a while. Annabelle and Eammon were floating too.

20

LIGHTNESS

Breathing fully and filling the body with light eliminates darkness and heaviness.

The atmosphere had changed somewhat at Los Monteros. Although Juan tried hard to act normal, he had lost his reference point. He struggled with the mundane and all small conversation seemed like a waste of breath. He knew it was only a stage in his development though, he had a feeling everything would settle down and he hoped he would soon begin living in a new and more productive way.

His father noticed his preoccupation and asked him several times if he was feeling alright. The brothers teased him, ignorant in their misdiagnosis of him just being homesick.

Juan, in truth was preoccupied. He was frantically planning his escape from the house to the threshing fields. He thought of little else. If he didn't get there he knew he would miss, well he didn't actually know what he would miss, and that was worse.

It would only take his dad to say they were taking a trip out somewhere, a light lunch, or even an afternoon in, playing cards, and the loose arrangement would be undone. That thought was a colossal weight which almost rooted him. I say almost because just as despair was about to embed its cruel claws, it suddenly struck him that if Alfonso was good for his money, true to his word, he should be able to apply one of his techniques to resolve his debilitating predicament.

He walked through the house and sat himself down on the patio, offering himself to the mountains. Softly closing his eyes he began to visualise the centre below his navel. He then tried his best to put the problem there and allow the universe to deal with it, like Alfonso had said, to transform it, to bring light where darkness menacingly dwelt.

Stretching up as much as he could and breathing slowly and deeply for a few minutes made him feel that at least he done something positive with the desperate dilemma.

On standing he did notice that he felt somewhat lighter and brighter, well he thought he did, subtle thing sometimes. He strolled into the house and began a conversation with his father.

"We go home the day after tomorrow," he informed him.

"Yes we do. Have you enjoyed your vacation son?"

"I have, I'm glad we chose here. Would we be able to come back one day?" he said, shocking his father with the unexpected appearance of enthusiasm. It pleased him to know his son had really had a good time after all, despite some strange behaviour which had left him bewildered at times. It's all most parents need to be content you know, just some recognition that their children are happy.

"Yes of course we can, we could bring your mum and your sister too," he added, encouraged by the tiny piece of positivism he had been shown.

"That would be nice; I think they would love it here too." Juan said, equally exalted by the pleasant exchange of words and feelings. He was inspired enough to consider asking if he could go for another walk tomorrow, almost carried away in the moment, then he suddenly steeled himself. He couldn't bear the thought of a negative at that moment, the security of hope was something he could relish a little longer. He would see if things swung his way naturally first.

21

DIMENSIONS

With sight, hearing, taste, smell and touch, we naively believe we know all about our world.

Jack and Florence were in close contact with Juan, tuning their dials one way, then the next, making sure their support was unfailing through his transformation, assisting his own guide Soran with tireless loyalty. Annabelle got regular visits too, full advantage taken of their cosmic communication capabilities, a phenomenon you will soon be seeing again of inter dimensional travel, which was once a naturally occurring event on your planet Earth too. Well that's until a carefully executed removal of all things esoteric saw the expansion of the human being deliberately denied and sufficiently suppressed by the rulers of your world, so much so you have gone from astral travel and telepathy to texting and emails. That's some communication breakdown.

Something else too, in case you didn't know already, you've been lied to about your origins, look at your temples and prolific ancient monuments; the stories are set in stone there. The Temple of Seti 1 in Abydos, Egypt, is a great place to start, but most temples throughout the world which have stories engraved in them will show you the truth of your origins. You can also go to a sacred mount in Iraq where you'll find incredible information on the origins of our planet. Oh sorry, just remembered they put a U.S. military base on top of it now, just a coincidence though, they are only fighting against terrorism of course. We have a great view from up here you know, we know what really goes on.

Their friendship (Jack and Florence's, sorry about the side track) with Soran had become a close one, their mutual interest in Juan's welfare being the cause; well I suppose it would really. As their trust in each other grew he had shown them how to access another dimension, one which had left a great impression on them. They visited there, oh many times I think, craving the intensity, a thousand times more than anything they had experienced before, floating through an expanse of absolute freedom. Words are too restrictive at this level of course as the freedom they felt there cannot rationally be described, not really. But travelling through that pulsating and vibrant blue experience, just for a few seconds, brings about an instant understanding of universal concepts. You could lose your mind in there, which would be great of course, because that's when you come to your senses. It's no wonder is it that they entered the portal more and more, grateful to Soran for showing them the opportunity to bathe in the purity of love and light, and agreeing, without any doubt, that Delmore would love it too, when he eventually came home.

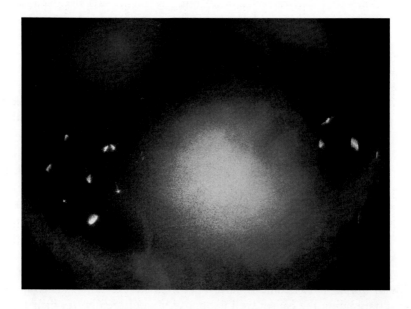

22

DREAMS

Maybe the closest thing to truth we have.

Alfonso was floating through the air just above head height, shouting instructions to Juan, but it was all too inaudible. Every time he got close enough to hear, a great gust of wind sent Alfonso up to the clouds once more. It went on and on like this for what seemed like an eternity. Juan, not being able to reach him, but not being able to walk away either.

The sun was turned up full, bathing Juan's bedroom in intense light. He woke from the dream only to realise the actual situation he was now in, had in fact been mirrored in his dream. Or perhaps visa versa.

He pulled open the blinds and looked across the street and up in the direction of Aljibe. Although it wasn't visible from the house, he was half hoping to see Alfonso floating somewhere out there. And somewhere out there was a world he had to escape to later on. Los Monteros was now a prison and the jailor was his own imploding negativity.

He closed the blinds and chose the clothes he was to escape in, khaki shirt for camouflage, full length track suit bottoms for protection on the walk, and his running shoes for, well, he couldn't be sure really. Suitably attired he headed out to the kitchen, all casual now, due to the suspicion he wrongly assumed he was creating, met his brothers and his dad and dealt with the first hurdle of breakfast.

"Good morning son, what do you want to do today? It's your last full day here."

Juan couldn't form the words that would decide his fate. He just mumbled, "anything dad," instantly cursing his own stupidity.

"Maybe you can take us on that walk of yours?" he suggested.

And there it was, the worst possible outcome had arrived within a minute or two of him waking. It would have been a disaster had his dad took them out for the day, but this scenario was even worse. Not only would he not get to see Alfonso alone for the final time, but he could be there waiting for him when they all walked through his mountain territory. His dad would see Alfonso and surely find out that he and Juan had been meeting each other in secret. Juan's heart sank, his head whirled and his nightmare manifested over a muted breakfast.

Things had suddenly become too grown up for him, after all he hadn't asked for any for it. Less than two weeks ago he was a carefree boy with no responsibilities, now he had the problems of the world to resolve, information that most humans will never acquire in their whole lives, plus the added responsibility of what to do with it. And yet here he was, powerless to even influence a simple meeting with Alfonso.

He struggled with his cereal, pointlessly pushing the corn flakes around the bowl, picking them up with his spoon and then tipping them back in the milk to watch them drown.

Outside his brothers were playing football and making all the usual noise of happy, carefree children, devoid of responsibility. The appealing scurry of young nonchalance registered with Juan and intensified his misery.

The white ceramic bowl with the heroic toreador embossed around the lip was morosely pushed away, and Juan, the pusher of the bowl, headed to the bathroom. Looking in the mirror, the one with the fingerprints of three brother's hands, he was surprised to find such a young boy staring back. He washed his face with much more vigour than was necessary for the task, as though a certain amount of rinses would wash away his predicament. The predicament of course could not be washed away, but neither was it remotely as bad as Juan imagined. Not when you think that his dad could easily have been reassured that Alfonso was not the maniac they thought, and just a few words exchanged would have soon sorted that one. In the head of Juan though, mystery and deceit reigned.

The morning dragged on and Juan, unsettled and tetchy, packed away a few things for the day of departure. He thought about asking his father to get some paint and a brush for him, a small consolation with a bigger contingency plan, but realised he had left it all too late.

His brothers had given up on coaxing him out for a game of football and his reluctance to join in generally had reaffirmed to them that he was undoubtedly the weirdo of the holiday.

Dad went and arrived back from the local shop with bread and cheese for their lunch. On the short walk back, short but sufficiently picturesque to induce thoughts of the romantic kind, he had thought about his wife Lucila and their daughter Alba. Usually it was the simple things that did it like folding clothes or hanging out the boys' washing to dry, the kind of jobs which Lucila adored doing, pegging out with a pride and purpose he could never match. Not that he took her for granted, he expressed his gratitude often, and the mere fact that Lucila knew that he always watched how she made the seemingly trivial a work of art was enough reward for her. He had sighed with the mmm of an outward breath as he thought about seeing them both tomorrow.

His day dream was short lived however; a loud knock at the front door responsible, jolting him from the coast to the mountains in a split second. Juan dashed to see who it was but his dad's adrenalin saw him out of the blocks first. Disappointment once more disturbed the fragile mood of Juan, the knock only belonging to the owner of the property, coming to collect the payment for the rental of Los Monteros. What he would have said if it would have been Alfonso there, he had no idea.

"It's only me," she said, making her way inside the house. "I hope you all enjoyed your stay and of course Methina Fondales itself?"

"It's been wonderful," said dad, knowing none of his sons would consider answering. "You are very privileged to wake up here every morning," he added for politeness.

"Yes we are, and I promise we never take it for granted."

"I'm not sure the scenery would allow for the unappreciative," he returned.

"Anyway, what are you going to do with your last day, surely you won't be staying in?"

Juan edged his way back to a place within earshot.

"I think we may all go out for a walk this afternoon, take in the last of its beauty you know. We have done a lot of walking already and Juan has even found a nice one on his own, you can show us later Juan?" he said louder, so Juan had to engage.

"Yes," came the usual monosyllabic response young boys produce when they are forced to talk in the presence of strange elders.

Dad settled the bill with the jovial lady who promised she would come and visit them in the morning before their departure, the jovial lady who set off through the door and stopped suddenly in her tracks.

"Oh I just remembered something. I don't know if any of your boys are interested in art, but someone left a beautiful painting set in the house and I haven't got a contact number for them. There is lots of paper too; it seems such a waste to do nothing with it, it looks like a really good set. Let me go and get it from the car."

He didn't have the heart to tell her none of them painted; she seemed to have made her mind up someone would be the beneficiary anyway.

A rejuvenated Juan peeped through the window to see if Alfonso was anywhere around. He saw the lady coming back with a box under her arm and tried to stay calm and breathe deeply. Then he casually strolled into the kitchen where he opened four cupboard doors and the fridge before closing them all again. She came back in the house and he froze beside the freezer.

"Hurry up and speak," he said to himself, desperate to know if he could hear her from his makeshift hideout.

"Here it is," she said loud and clear. "It is a good one isn't it? There are some brushes too; you may as well have it all."

"It looks great, I'm certain one of them will use it, probably Juan, he's the arty one. Great musician you know."

"At least it will come to some use now. I really must be on my way; I have to meet a dear friend of mine. Don't forget I'll be back in the morning to say goodbye," she said, leaving nothing to respond with apart from "goodbye."

The father stood there looking at the art set she had thrust upon him.

"Juan, where are you?"

Juan crouched down and remained silent. Then he realised he had no reason to hide from anyone and wondered what his mind was playing at.

"Coming," he shouted.

"Look here Juan, the owner has left this for us," he said, the box already opened up and being displayed in the manner of a hopeful salesman. "I wondered if perhaps you might like it."

Juan wondered how to play his next card. Too much enthusiasm may look a little suspect, not enough and it may get offered to his brothers.

"Yes I'd love it," he replied, with too much enthusiasm.

"Here you go son, see what you can come up with."

"I'll go and put it in my room, thank you dad."

"Don't thank me; thank the lady when you see her tomorrow."

"I will," he said, from the third stair up, already on his way to his bedroom to inspect his little miracle.

He shut the bedroom door behind him and laid it out on the bed. The case was a work of art in itself, top quality mahogany with dovetail joints and wooden dividers inside. Juan tried to look at all the colours at once, scanning them to see if any matched the colour of the mountains. He shut the lid and opened it again, as though he would find something different in there. There was a section of brushes of varying widths. Carefully lifting one out, he made a few imaginary strokes on imaginary canvas with a real imagination. It had been more than a year since his last painting, a high standard one in fairness, but having dropped the subject at school after being forced to choose either music or art, he had never developed his potential any further.

He looked at the set for the best part of twenty minutes. As the excitement eased off the burning question of how it had got to him went full throttle, flat out, full steam ahead, I think you'd say. Well after researching your Earth dialect of course, as I have, checking with my thesaurearth too.

Had one of his guides arranged it? Was it just coincidence? Hadn't Alfonso said there was no such thing as coincidence? He couldn't remember now. The good news was at least he had his chance to paint, coincidence or synchronicity? Again, I'll have to leave that to you.

He felt some relief at least from his previous torment. It wasn't the perfect outcome, granted, but he felt a connection to Alfonso never the less. He broke out into a huge grin as he thought about finishing his painting and secretly taking it to Aljibe for Alfonso. It would be an opportunity to explain why his dad and brothers were with him on the walk. He was sure he would be able to sneak out in the morning to offer an enthusiastic apology.

The day suddenly had a renewed urgency about it, get the walk over with, deal with Alfonso waiting in the field, if he's there, paint the picture and drop it off in the morning. Things seemed good again; someone must be watching and helping after all.

Juan lay on the bed and thought about everything that had happened to him, and it smothered him in truth. Part of him wanted to just fall asleep and wake up from a dream. The reality of his new world suddenly surged up from his bowels and terrified him. He wrestled to push it back but it rose defiantly up to his chest, through his throat and rested at his screwed up eyes. He put his head in his arms and cried, every emotion suddenly erupting, a volcano of sadness, relief, fear, loneliness, tension, and all of those emotions seizing the opportunity to turn themselves into tears. His young body shook as the beast of darkness temporarily possessed him. He thought of his mum and how much he needed her there to soothe away the terror.

It took ten minutes before the last sob had left him. It felt like ten hours. He couldn't believe no-one had heard him. Exhausted and empty, but relieved that he didn't have to explain himself to anyone; he walked over to the mirror and checked his reflection. Apart from red eyes he was the same boy. He knew in his heart all he had been told was true and he also knew he would be strong enough to deal with it. He still loved his world and was determined to play his part in writing the ending. He had cried at the death of his old life, then staring once more at the boy looking back, said goodbye to it for ever.

23

POSTURE

It is difficult to keep universal connection when you are bent like a banana. Or is it?

Juan led the way out of the village, a reluctant rambler repeating facts such as, "there really isn't anything of interest to see," and "it's only a slightly different way to Busquistar." He hoped as he walked that Alfonso possessed enough common sense among his infinite wisdom to ignore him if he saw them walking.

"Slow down Juan," David shouted.

Juan tried, but the tension in him would not allow for strolling. Strolling is for the sedentary, those who have lived through and come out the other side of their problems, and dashing, that was for those just entering those quagmires. They left the village and were soon heading out through the trees and shrubs, with Juan, still rushing and now straining his eyes through the miniature forest, trying desperately to see further than was logical. It took them another five minutes to emerge from the density of the trees. Juan's eagle eyes were scanning the area up to a hundred yards in front of them, left to right and back again, over and over. The rock, once mystical, now miserable, crept slowly into view, the same rock where his lecture had taken place only two days ago. It was empty now and devoid of life, as though its only purpose in a million years had been to provide support for one seemingly random meeting, then discarded like a redundant prop from a film set.

"Remember the guy with the stick there?" David said.

"I do," replied José.

"He sure knew how to use that sword. I wish we would have got to know him, I bet he was really interesting."

"He might have chopped us up and boiled us in a cauldron," David laughed, ever the dramatist.

Juan kept quiet; he didn't like them talking about his friend like that. He felt like giving them a snippet of his new found knowledge, a lash of Alfonso's allegorical offerings, but he knew he must keep it to himself, at least for a while.

They carried on walking with Juan, his head hung like a condemned man to a rope, leading them out to the threshing field.

The father suggested they sit on the rock and rest a while, before the trek over to Busquistar. Juan's brothers offered no resistance to the idea and the rock had a purpose once more.

All four of the Santiago family managed to squash on, despite the acute angles and shortage of a moss free and flat surface. Juan suddenly felt enlivened, remembering his little meditation and his lesson about calling his spirit guides for guidance. He thought about being in the centre of the universe, about his posture and his breathing. He observed his brother's and his father's postures and could see, albeit with complete absence of criticism, just what Alfonso had meant. He smiled to himself and felt the inner tingling of renewed hope. He felt even more hopeful too when Alfonso was nowhere to be seen, the relief of his absence taking the initial glory, yet at the same time, disappointment and concern as to why he hadn't turned up loitered arrogantly, refusing their runners up medals. It was, in fact, the relief that won temporarily, but the disappointment and concern eventually carried a handle each of the trophy.

They reached, after resting on the rock, the beautiful village of Busquistar and enthusiastically unpacked their sandwiches and drinks. Juan tried some polite conversation, aware of the fact he had been almost silent throughout the walk. And for once he actually appreciated his brothers, even though it was only for the fact that they had enough ability to do small talk all day if necessary. Dad gathered discarded tin foil and told the sons to breathe in the fresh air, the way dads always do.

"Make the most of it," he said. "We can't take it home with us."

Juan's attention had already shifted, pulled to the hypnotic sound of bells, bells that mountain goats wear around their necks, jangling in the far off distance. The noise eventually disappeared and he found himself tuning into the buzzing of a bee somewhere closer before the drone of a light aircraft won the decibel race.

When the tension and fear he had previously been carrying slowly abated, he realised that his senses had been heightened somehow. He realised he was beginning to feel much more alive and aware of his environment. He knew the world hadn't changed, well not the outside world, so he surmised it was the way he was viewing it that was different. Mundane moments would be few and far between from now on. The change had come from within; the only place the world can change from.

24

NATURE

If you focus on the beautiful complexities of a plant structure, you will see the great power of nature at its best, a universe within a universe.

They left the village, stopping only briefly to admire the last house on the hill, well the garden really, boasting some of the most exotic plants and flowers mountainous Spain had to offer. Ten sunflowers on guard duty ran along side the fence at the bottom of the garden, dutifully checking the comings and goings of the valley below. There were many other flowers too, each one unique, each one also part of the one.

Juan gently pulled one of the flowers towards him, staring into the head of the plant and losing himself in its intricacies and incredible patterns. His father brought him out again with a swift prod to the rib.

"Look at this," he pleaded. "Just look at it dad."

"It's very nice son, we have seen them before though."

"I know but look dad, look at all those yellow balls, they spiral don't they? Spiral into its centre, makes you feel like you could fall into it doesn't it? How does it do it dad? Look at the perfect petals too; I've never noticed just how perfect they are."

"Yes it is wonderful when you look at it that way son. You observe things well. Shall we head back now?" he said, not being able to resist another look, partially embarrassed by his own previous ignorance.

He put his arm around his wonderful son and squeezed him in, appreciating the minute but monumental moment he had just witnessed. Together they all made the walk back through the valley, through the trees, past the rock and into Methina Fondales once more. Juan tried not to think about why Alfonso had not shown. He would never know by thought alone. Maybe it would be resolved before they left tomorrow, or even some time after, at a point in a future that was becoming increasingly unpredictable. But for now he chose to focus on the painting he wanted so much to do. He packed the remainder of his clothes as soon as they got to Los Monteros, and within an hour he was sat on the terrace with his new box snugly sitting on his knee.

25

EXPRESSION

You don't need to be an artist, a musician, a dancer or actor to be creative. Be true to your unique self and your whole life can be an art form.

There is a truth in the saying, "a picture is worth a thousand words." You can say something on canvas which would never be possible with the pretension of strained vocabulary. Feelings locked away for years easily released within the swirls and swoops of the brush, sadness in the dark colours and joy in the light, each time beginning with a clean canvas and ending up where no one else would. The adventure belongs to you and you are expressing your personal story. No two people are exactly alike. No two artists can paint in the same way.

Juan would soon discover these truths. He set out his paints on the terrace table and tried to empty his mind of everything that had happened to him in the last two weeks. It wasn't just the information he had received that had caused his transformation; Alfonso had affected him at the very core of his existence.

The brush and the hand of Juan soon harmonised, sometimes sprinting across the paper and filling large portions of mountainside in one sweep, other times painstakingly poking and dotting around, laboriously filling in the minor details. He was totally absorbed in the activity, transfixed and temporarily removed from normality, his head moving from mountain to paper over and over again.

His family assessed the seriousness of the situation and left him to complete his mission. Exactly what it was they didn't know, but they had seen that determined look on his face before, they knew it was best to leave him to it.

Finally, three and a half hours later, Juan wandered into the house looking tired at best, demented at worst. He was physically and mentally spent and collapsed on the armchair, sinking down through the seat into a sleep fifteen minutes in length and a thousand feet deep. The picture that was about to shape the rest of his life was done, drying outside and waiting only for attention to bring it to life.

Amazement swam in the eyes of his Father, as disbelief anchored him and shame showed him a son he realised he hardly knew.

"Juan . . . how did you . . . when . . . I mean, I had no idea. It's incredible . . . get your brothers quick," he said, still staring at the painting he was holding like an heir loom dinner plate, eventually putting it down on the dining table and hugging his son.

"What are you going to do next?" he asked Juan, who was already struggling to see how he would get this one to Alfonso and explain its disappearance.

26

ACTION

Make a choice, follow its path and don't look back. It's only a different route to the same destination.

The silence of their last mountain morning lost graciously to excited chatter, car doors opening and closing, and castors dragged on concrete. Juan had actually woken an hour before anyone else. He casually let himself out and ran up to Aljibe with the painting rolled up in his hand, knowing there would be no time to talk to Alfonso, even if he was up and about. He quietly pushed it through the letter box and convinced himself that it was the best thing to do. As he walked back to Los Monteros he had a feeling it wasn't quite the end with Alfonso.

27

LEAVING

Make sure you leave every experience richer than you came to it.

The journey home was a huge contrast to the one that brought them here just two weeks ago. Same trusty old Renault plodding out of Methina Fondales, granted, and the same rattle of the exhaust with the missing bracket, of course. Even the same aroma of the three year old vanilla essence air freshener shaped like a tree and hanging determinedly on the mirror, same dusty roads and same views through dusty windows, naturally. But a very changed human being sat in the back, passenger side, observing such things. Juan was the great change, looking back through the rear window at the mysterious aura which seemed to be hanging over Methina.

This tiny village had welcomed him with open arms, slapped him in the face, shook him vigorously to release all out dated beliefs, and then finally nursed him like a baby. He felt the strange mixture of sadness and optimism as the village faded from his life.

As they approached Aljibe, Juan half expected Alfonso to be waving at the door. He wasn't though and the building just looked sad and shrouded in loneliness. He thought about Alfonso and how later he would be busy cooking and serving people in there with his economical movements and gifted conversation, nutrition for starters, enlightenment for the main course, and a bowl of purification for pudding. All of that life going on in there, yet the building on the outside was dead wood and bricks, like a relationship that ends and the rooms of the marital home have had the life force sucked out of them, as though the love between two people is the very life support of the house, and when it leaves it takes colours, shapes, and vibrancy with it.

Juan eventually turned around and looked once more through the front windscreen to face his unknown future.

The Renault rattled on the rough roads that led them out of Methina, small villages soon being replaced with bigger ones as the road spiralled outwards, modestly becoming a motorway, devoid of any beauty and only intent on keeping things moving quickly. Juan was happy to be back on the coastal road at Motril; he loved the spectacular drive along side the ocean towards Algarrobo. He didn't think that he had missed the sea and the beach, yet the pleasure he felt on seeing them indicated otherwise. He thought about his mum and sister and felt joy again, knowing they were about to be reunited very soon. His joy climbed a notch to excitement as they eventually turned off the coast road and took the sign post for Algarrobo and Sayalonga. He smiled as the car rattled on the old roads, past the poly tunnels and round the hairpin bend. The wheels skidded as they had done a thousand times before, on the last hill with the shiny road surface, gripping eventually and rolling on to where the old men of the village congregated to share wonderful stories of whole lives spent in one village. Some of them waved and others just lazily nodded their approval at the family's return. Only one bend to go now, small squeals as hot tyres greeted hot tarmac, four grinning mouths containing the smugness of a mission almost achieved. Juan felt the excitement run through the blood in his young veins. He was still a child after all and he felt utter relief at the realisation. The small child with a huge spirit was home and the hug; fragranced with familiarity, lasted long enough for him to be bathed in comfort. He would have stayed there for hours if it wasn't for mum having to distribute herself evenly. His worries fell like bricks from an overcoat pocket, leaving him with only one, the feeling he would lift right off the ground when his mum finally let go.

28

TRAGEDY

Tragedy comes to all of us. How you deal with it will be down to the philosophy you own today.

"At least we had a few years of happiness," Annabelle said, searching for words to wipe out the horror of the situation they now owned. There were no words however.

The three of them sat with their individual pain and a collective numbness, united in grief yet paradoxically, never more alone.

Colleen had been staying with Eammon's parents since the day it happened, with Eammon nipping backwards and forwards to see her, bravely trying to force feed normality to the closed mouth of reality. Annabelle could not find the strength to go, she felt anesthetised to the point of being unable to get to the car, let alone compose herself for the necessary protection of her daughter.

It had happened so fast, such a normal day, the morning spent at Roy and Margaret's house, the presents for Colleen's third birthday wrapped and hidden, the usual three teas and one coffee, the drawn out goodbyes at the gate before the last look back to wave at mum and dad, and then the short walk back to the cottage.

Annabelle had gone over it a hundred times already, trying to rewrite it in sheer desperation. And every time the cold fact that it wasn't a work of fiction but a truth set in stone delivered its brutal blow. That last wave symbolising the last time mum and dad would be seen together felt so callous to her, so devastatingly final, uncompromising and cruel, the way death always seems.

"A brain tumour," she had just made out through the hysteria of that telephone call, panic travelling down the wire, from a mouth to an ear and then processed via the brain to break down all systems.

It had been quick, they heard the word "blessing" many times and "the best way to go," clichéd sayings from caring people clutching at straws.

Roy's body was still slumped at the table when Annabelle and Eammon arrived, their proximity giving them an advantage over the emergency services. Annabelle rushed over to where her father lay, stopping just short of the table, a momentary pause while she assessed the unfamiliar predicament of what to do when you desperately need to hug someone who has vacated their body.

She noticed the unfinished cup of tea; the tea that had been poured while he was still living and had the audacity to still remain while Roy had gone. Her mum hugged her and the tears flowed without time limits.

"He was so happy with us wasn't he Eammon, here at the cottage, playing with Colleen and having us around all the time? She really loved her Grandad didn't she? All those happy times for dad, do you think he has taken them with him?"

"I'm sure he has love. He's probably still around her you know. They say that don't they?"

"Yes I bet he is. I just wish it could have lasted longer, just a bit more, that wouldn't have been too much to ask. I'll miss him so much, and our Colleen will too; I don't know what to tell her, we will have to say something soon though."

"I know love, we will work something out. Lets get this bit over with first; I think we will all feel a bit different then," he reassured her, not realising that for the next few weeks they would not feel the same from one moment to the next.

Three years they had been at the cottage. Three wonderful summers and three cosy cold winters by the crackling fire, Roy taking charge of all things flammable, and Colleen hopping from lap to lap for different types of love and affection, choosing carefully just what type of energy she needed.

She was blessed in a way that both parents and grandparents seemed to connect with the soul of Colleen. They did so naturally, unintentionally allowing her potential to unfold. They knew no other way. Colleen would cope with the situation better than the others. The sadness would pass quickly and when it did return from time to time she would not hold on to it. She could move her attention quickly and naturally to the moment she was in, being totally absorbed in that new situation. This is how all children live, masters of living in the moment. Adults have to re learn this simple truth by following gurus or enrolling on specialised courses, where if they are vigilant and pursue it long enough, they may learn how to act like a child.

29

CELEBRATIONS

As we mourn and suffer our losses, there are homecoming parties and much celebration elsewhere.

Roy was catching up with old friends and family, the realisation of his certain infinity causing him to leap from one old soul to the next, a single thought reuniting him with all of the people he had grieved over in his past.

It was his mum who came to meet him, her familiarity aiding the transition, the tunnel drawing him effortlessly to its paradise, colours pulsating and vibrant, and Roy, in absolute peace, offering no resistance to its lure.

The opportunity to review his life was available whenever he was ready; mistakes made, goals achieved, triumphs and unfulfilled dreams, a "to do" list to carry forward to his next trip. In the main he would see that he had experienced great love, given it in abundance and received it in abundance, leaving one loving situation and arriving in another.

The reflection took place in gardens inconceivable to the human mind, idyllic settings to quietly come to terms with the results of all the thought forms and actions of his latest trip out.

After the review, the gentle analysis, he began to think about the family he had left behind. He concentrated on Colleen and found himself entering her dimension via her dream state. He became aware that he could influence Colleen's dreams to a point where he could slip between dimensions to be with her, the realisation was another monumental one.

There they were, in the garden of the cottage in Mulranny, hugging each other beside the honey suckle. It was sunny in the dream and the garden was vibrant and intense. Roy smiled to himself at the never ending aspect of nature.

"I love you Colleen," he whispered, feeling the sunshine on his back, smelling the freshness of the newly cut grass, as much alive in that moment as he ever was as Roy the Human. The realisation that their love was also eternal iced his cosmic cake.

He held her face in his hands and felt the newness, the smoothness, and the softness of her skin. The rapture, sadly, was temporarily suspended as he noticed the face slowly beginning to change.

Around the eyes appeared faint lines which soon turned into deeper furrows, the hair became longer and darker and eventually turned to silver. The skin dropped from the bones and elongated the face, and he realised he was looking at Colleen as an old lady, the same spark in the eyes, the same beauty, the same love for each other, just a future vision of her in the now of no time, a future and past fusing into one moment, an awareness operating from a different set of rules completely. He knew with great conviction there was no where to go and nothing to learn. He had been all things and always will be all things, and it is all in the now. How futile all search for enlightenment. How laughable the pursuit of happiness. How silly he thought to worry about time and aging when it does not exist. How crazy to worry about dying when it does not happen. We come from the source and return to the source and all of us are linked to this source for eternity. His so called death had not happened; he was still here amongst his loved ones.

He tried to tell Colleen to enjoy every moment of her life here without fear. He gave up on the words and communicated it through feeling. Looking at her face once more it was the image of the three year old again. Her eyes brightened as the message was delivered. He hugged her and said "see you later," just because he knew he could.

His attention jumped once more to the spirit realm he knew already to be home. He was pulled away from Colleen and the garden to be enveloped in light, complete freedom, weightlessness and wisdom.

30

COPING

Children cope better than adults because they live more in the moment. They suffer the same but usually only once. Adults get stuck in the head area and repeat the cycle continuously.

"I saw Grandad Roy in my dream dad," Colleen said casually, as Eammon was bringing her back to the cottage to explain what had happened to Roy.

"What did he say?" Eammon answered, equally casually.

"He said he loved me. We were in the garden at our house."

Eammon seized the moment, took a breath and utilised the gift he had been presented with.

"Yes he does love you and I'm sure you will see him in your dreams again," he said reassuringly. "But he isn't at his house anymore sweetness, he has gone to another place and is very happy there. It's a wonderful place Colleen, but he can only come to see us in our dreams. Do you understand?"

And that was it. She understood enough. He had rehearsed it a hundred times, completely different to the explanation he had just given, but the opportunity arose and he had grabbed it gratefully.

After a few weeks Colleen stopped asking about her Grandad so much, and life once again began to have a hint of normality to it. Of course for Annabelle and Eammon the sadness came and went and pain was only ever a thought or a memory away, and unbeknown to Annabelle, so was her father.

A FEW YEARS LATER

Latif, Falak and their mum and dad were travelling once more, their love of art and architecture leading them to a region of Spain called

Granada, the intention (at least the intention of Hacham) being to absorb the beauty of the incredible building named "The Alhambra palace."

They boarded the ferry at Cueta and in less than an hour had docked in Algejeras. The coast road took them towards Marbella, pushing on through Malaga, Nerja and on as far as Motril.

Mum and Latif were jointly responsible for the map reading and collaborated to make perfect choices of the roads leading to Granada. By mid afternoon they were in their hotel taking the usual "just arrived" stroll around the hotel vicinity. From its high vantage point the hotel offered superb views across Granada, causing the simultaneous sigh at what was there, and of what was to come.

Breakfast the following morning saw them in the restaurant before most other guests had risen. They munched and planned their way through cereal, toast and coffee.

Hacham not wanting to get caught up in Spanish traffic had decided to leave their 4x4 in the hotel car park, taking a taxi to the Alhambra palace instead.

The literal translation of Alhambra is "The red fortress" and derives from the colour of the red clay of which the fort is made.

It dates back to the end of the Muslim rule in Spain in the mid 1300s and cleverly mixes natural elements with man made ones, a credit to the skill of the Muslim craftsmen of that period. The Muslim rulers however lost the Alhambra in 1492 without it even being attacked. Crafty King Ferdinand11 of Aragon and Queen Isabella of Castile took over all the surrounding areas with massive numbers. You really are a gruesome bunch down there, looking forward to joining you!

As interesting as its bloodied history was, Hacham's real interest lay in the architecture and artwork. The decoration of stiff conventional foliage, Arabic inscriptions and geometrical patterns wrought into the wonderful arabesques, led him to the precipice, while the abundance of beautiful hand painted tiles gently tipped him over.

Of all the things Hacham had read and all the stories he had heard from the people who had visited it, nothing could have prepared him for his visit. Mesmerised, bordering unsound, he rushed from one part to the next as if it would be demolished any minute. His family had to leave him to it after he refused to stop for lunch. By the end of his visit he was exhausted and looked strange to his family with his huge grin, large eyes and wild hair. He never stopped talking during the taxi ride and continued long into the night, at the expense of his over tolerant wife.

31

CHANCE

There is no such thing.

The holiday passed quickly, days freefalling into evenings and crumpled clothes slowly returning to open suitcases. On their penultimate day they decided to have a last drive around the Alpujarras, an unplanned "go where the road looks good," sort of drive. They cruised through the busy town of Lanjaron and on to the sleepy villages of Pampaneira and Pitres, stopping at many view points to utter the same words of amazement.

The sign post for Trevelez enticed them to visit its beautiful town at the peak of Las Alpujarras, ham curing capital of Spain, due to its, well, perfect ham curing climate. Every shop there utilised its ceiling space for the hanging of these huge chunks of meat, leaving shoppers to dodge the bizarre objects hanging from rafters to buy their souvenirs.

Trevelez, however was not to be. Hacham, tired through driving and a holiday with little relaxation, suggested reluctantly that they head slowly back in the direction of Granada, taking in as much scenery as they could on route, facilitating the forming of fond memories to take back to Morocco. The map readers however had long since retired and they found themselves in smaller and smaller villages.

"Shall we stop here for a drink and a little stretch?" mum said, intuitively verbalising the words that sat only as thought forms in the heads of the others.

"Good idea, we can ask for directions while we are there."

They stopped the car, slid out and walked with knee bending exaggeration towards the bar.

"Aljibe," Falak said as they walked inside. They chose a table near a window, Falak and Latif instinctively went to sit down, leaving mum and dad to sort menus and such.

"Good afternoon, I hope you will be dining with us here, and experience, if I may say, what is certainly the best home cooking for miles around," Alfonso said in almost perfect French.

"Well yes, I think we will," replied mum, won over by his language skills, acute observation and confident sales patter. "Do you have a menu?"

"Yes it is I, Alfonso." he said, before flawlessly listing all the food available, including the full ingredients and benefits of each meal. "My recommendation today would be, and only by pure chance, the Moroccan vegetables served on a bed of spicy couscous."

"That sounds great," Hacham added.

"It comes with a money back guarantee and I make it all myself you know, one spoon of joy, two of friendship and a generous sprinkle of vitamin glee," he laughed to himself, counting out invisible scoops. "Now please be seated while I bring you some drinks over, dehydration is prohibited here I'm afraid."

"Thank you," Hacham said. "And may I ask where you learned to speak such good French?"

"Language is the expression of thought, feeling, and emotion too. A momentous responsibility wouldn't you say? I try to learn as many as I can. Serving people as you know is difficult to do without good communication. Service applies to much more than food, in my opinion. Yes, French, I learned from a two year stay in Avignon. I studied the graceful art of Aikido there with a great Master from Japan. He taught me to train like a warrior and laugh like a child. Now let me get some water for you and your very patient family, they seem to be admiring my painting there; it was given to me by an old friend."

Mum and dad joined their children at the table. A minute later Alfonso appeared with a jug of iced water.

"What do you think of it then?"

"The colours are fantastic," Latif said, "very unusual."

Hacham studied the painting with his own eyes of expertise.

"It certainly is incredible. Who did you say did it?"

"Juan Santiago is the name, never even signed it, and the incredible thing is that this was his first serious painting. Apart from a few bits at school he had done nothing, and he was only fourteen at the time, six years ago now. What do you think about that?"

"I thought you said he was an old friend."

"Yes a few centuries we go back, do you like it?"

"Yes I like it," he replied, choosing to evade the "few centuries ago" comment. "Are you still in contact with him?"

"He lives on the coast, a village by the name of Algarrobo. I only ever met him the once. My home is here in these mountains you see. I don't travel and the boy, well he's too busy for an old timer like me I suppose. But I know one day we will meet again, I do know that much. Would you like to buy a painting from him? I can give you his address, though I can't be certain he's even painted anything since."

"Maybe I will call in on him on our way home. I am an art dealer funnily enough."

"What a coincidence," he added, traces of sarcasm growing across his face.

"I buy from all around the world. Buy, sell, and unfortunately, obsessively collect. I have a vast collection of art I just can't part with. It would be interesting to see if he has pursued his talent further."

"Yes, yes, go and see him, Algarrobo is only one hour and forty five minutes away. You must go, you simply must," he said, the notion of a possible reunion causing the temporary change in pitch. "And I also must go and prepare your nutrition for the day."

"What an interesting little place. I'm so glad we got lost," Mum said quietly.

Falak and Latif were still staring at the painting when Alfonso appeared once more with the food. They felt a strong connection with it but had no idea why.

"Please be seated," Alfonso said, pulling off a stereo typical waiter pose. "You can admire it some more later, but first you must all eat."

He disappeared briefly before making a grand re entrance and proudly presenting their lunch.

"How tasty it is," the father managed in between mouthfuls. The agreements came in nods and groans, mouths too preoccupied to speak. It's fair to say that hardly a word was spoken for the next few minutes, apart from answering Alfonso's periodic and rhetorical question, "is everything alright?"

He left them alone a good ten minutes after they had finished eating before appearing with a bottle of red wine and a huge grin.

"Please accept a glass on the house. It's organic of course, promoting merriment without destroying health."

"Thank you so much, you are most generous," Zahra said, refusal not being an option. "And by the way the food was delicious. We won't be asking for our money back," she said with confidence, now the foundations of joviality had been firmly laid.

"That is excellent; now let us drink a toast to the friendship between the Spanish and the Moroccans. It's hard to believe our communication level at one time was with weapons and hatred. Now we sit here as fellow humans, putting right hundreds of years of wrongdoing, breaking down barriers and blending borders, merging mindsets and melting hatred. Never under estimate what far reaching consequences one well meaning toast can have."

With that said, he stood up proudly and added this, "To a new future."

The family felt obligated to repeat the phrase, although they couldn't have meant it anymore genuinely than they did. Alfonso had certainly woken up their emotions in his little restaurant. Millions of people spend small fortunes and large chunks of time travelling to sacred places; meeting revered guru's who pick their pockets as they kiss their feet, while others just wander into a simple village restaurant, order lunch and have their lives changed forever.

Before long, and quicker than any of them would have wished, Alfonso was saying goodbye to the family who had gotten slightly lost. They certainly had more direction now though.

Alfonso gave the father Juan's address in Algarrobo.

"Look the boy up," he shouted after them.

"We will," they answered, looking back as Alfonso grew smaller and smaller, still waving, until he was only a dot making sure his guests had truly gone.

32

OLD FRIENDS

All friends are old friends.

Villages in Spain draw you in on big roads which cunningly turn into little side streets, ambitious alleyways and then glorified ginnels, and before you know what's what, they are squeezing you tighter and tighter as you near the centre, leaving you with the fear that you will be crushed to death for daring to enter. That's what they do.

Not for the first time they found themselves lost in one of these shrinking villages. The streets of Algarrobo have not been designed; they have been thrown together with the care free abandon that too much sunshine brings.

They called in a coffee bar, smiling profusely and intuitively to defuse the certain attention strangers always create in the village intimacy of their café's, showing an elderly man engrossed in a café latte the slip of paper with Juan's address on. Very quickly they were engaged in the interaction of over emphasised words and manic hand gestures, discovering with great relief they were only one street away from Juan.

They left the coffee bar and climbed the steep steps to the top of the street. A left turn, past the house with all the plants outside, then a quick look up to the right and there was the house of Juan, perfect directions derived from hopeful hand gestures.

They stood there surveying the layout of the house; finally working out that the front door was around the side, they approached it with a collective bout of anxiety.

"Go on then, knock," mum urged, as if who ever did knock would have to take full responsibility for whatever consequences came. So dad knocked.

They heard the click of heels across a tiled floor, then the clang of an iron bolt and the slow drawn out squeak, which revealed a classic looking lady, black dress, hair tied up, emphasising beautiful strong features.

"Hello," Lucila said, surveying the foursome with caution and curiosity.

Dad took a deep breath and began looking for the simplest Spanish words to quickly explain why four Moroccan strangers would be on her doorstep.

"We are looking for Juan, does he live here?"

"Yes he does, what has he done?" his mother asked, already counting at least three acts of rebellion he may have been guilty of.

"Nothing bad, I have come to talk to him about his paintings. We saw one of them in a restaurant in Las Alpujarras; the owner gave us his address," he said, holding the piece of paper out for her to see, just in case she didn't believe him.

"In Las Alpujarras you say?"

"Yes we met a gentleman there. He was a great admirer of your son's work actually. That's why I have come. I am an art dealer from Morocco you see."

"You better come in then," she said, not really any clearer and cutting the conversation conveniently short.

The four of them entered the house and stood in the lounge waiting for the next instruction, being inside somehow magnifying their feelings of vulnerability.

"One moment, I think he is on the roof," she said, pointing up several times to clarify her statement.

"Sit down while I go and see."

They entered the house and headed for the bright orange sofa, sneakily surveying the lounge in the same manner everyone does on a first visit to someone's home. They saw a small television on top of a table in the corner; a television which also served as a lamp stand and displayed one with no shade. There was an antique bookcase against the main wall which had been there for at least three generations, still in perfect condition while the books and its various owners had long turned to dust. Hacham saw a few paintings on the far wall and was straining to see if they were the work of Juan, too respectful to get up and look at them without permission.

They spoke in whispers about the house as the mother's heels clicked up the iron staircase and onto the roof of the house. A minute later she appeared with Juan, who also looked shocked to find four Moroccans on his sofa.

"They are here about those paintings you do," she said, making sure the guests were clear that painting had nothing to do with her. "I'll go and make some tea."

Hacham stood up and walked towards Juan, hand offered out for shaking, mind searching for Spanish words he hadn't used in a long time.

"Hello, my name is Hacham. I am an art dealer and I saw one of your paintings in Methina Fondales. It was in a restaurant there."

He stopped speaking for a moment to see if the Spanish delivered had been received as intended.

Juan nodded to confirm he had understood, the nod contained enough inspiration for Hacham to continue. Juan's mum banged pots, shook her head, and muttered and mused at her son's secrecy.

"I really liked the picture and wondered if you are still painting?"

Juan placed his hand across his mouth, as if some peculiar noise would have escaped if he hadn't. The confirmation that his picture had been received and was actually hanging in Alfonso's restaurant caught him completely off guard, the six years between the two events proving to be insufficient preparation.

"Oh, I do still paint but don't sell too many, only to the people of this village. I wouldn't know where to start beyond that. Has Alfonso sent you? How is he? Is he still working?" he said with growing curiosity.

"Yes he's fine, he told me to visit you, I called on the off chance."

Mum interrupted the conversation with a tray of tea and her best cups for the Moroccan guests. Hacham would have drunk from a bucket if he could have had a minted tea like back home, though he graciously accepted what had been presented.

"I would like to help you if I can, the painting I saw, well it's worthy of any gallery. If you could show me some more of your pictures I may be able to get you an exhibition where you can sell your work."

Juan composed himself, the words gallery and exhibition had thrown him a little, paint on the brush of any aspiring artist.

"I don't know if they are what you are looking for. I don't know about commercial painting at all. You're welcome to come and see though; they are just in my bedroom."

Hacham followed Juan, a mixture of hope and trepidation in every arriving step that the paintings would be good, especially now they had got this far, an apology would be nothing short of a tragedy. Juan scrabbled around under his bed and came up with a huge folder which was opened almost apologetically but met with an approving smile.

They were more than good enough and would cause a sensation when they were eventually displayed in the contemporary art gallery off the Grand Socco in Tangiers.

"They are wonderful," he said, genuinely. "We can certainly display these. Let me go back home and see what I can arrange, I will telephone you soon. If all goes to plan I can come over and collect you, you may have to stay with me for a week or so if that is ok. Have you ever been to Morocco?"

"No never, that's really exciting," Juan said, trying to keep elation suppressed.

"I can show you my own collection when you come over too, I'm sure you will love them. Oh where are my manners? Please let me introduce my family, my excitement has made me ignorant. This is my wife Zahra, and these are my children, Latif and Falak."

He shook their hands and made easy conversation with Falak and Latif. They had a better understanding of Spanish than their father, Falak being the most fluent. They said they wished they could paint like Juan. Juan said he was looking forward to seeing Morocco. He asked about their house, he had no idea what a palace it was and they were modest in their description.

Conversation extended through tea and biscuits. The mother had now joined them, finally giving in to her curiosity. Addresses and phone numbers were exchanged, a collection of Juan's works were taken, and another little piece of art history was born. And even more incredibly Robert, Kitty and Delmore had found each other, a three dimensional coincidence or a universal given, depending only on perception.

They sat there chatting and laughing as they had done a thousand times before, and will do a thousand times more, carrying their eternal spirit from one world to the next. And now on a planet of more than six billion souls they were once more reunited. A seemingly impossible fate, and yet every day the seemingly impossible happens. As they said goodbye in Algarrobo they felt that connection, as though they had known each other far longer than an hour. That same feeling everyone has now and again and wrongly assume they are meeting for the first time.

33

COFFEE AND CONSPIRACY

The truth is coming out. We are waking up on a mass scale. Keep an open mind and some concrete boots.

Juan carried on painting, waiting patiently for the call from Morocco. He had enough orders to keep him solvent and didn't need to work as such, mostly being asked to paint people's houses in the unusual style he had become known and respected for. Work also came from bars and restaurants, buildings imaginatively captured and displayed by life long licensees, proud of the part they played within in the bricks and mortar they sweated in every day.

Juan's heart was never really in it, he much preferred to use his vision to make his universal mind tangible on canvas. This is what really stimulated him, a thought or a feeling that could transfer to colour, shade and structure, a passion passed on from the heart, through the bristles of a brush and finally onto paper.

He spent a lot of his time in Malaga now, a half hour journey by car or bus, never train though, an irrational fear of them had seen him avoiding tracks for almost a decade, a fear which he planned to conquer one day.

The buzz of the city made him feel alive and he loved it as much as the stillness and silence of the country. Most of his friends were students of the university in Malaga, many of them studying art themselves and although they had tried many times to convince Juan to join them, he held steadfast to his principles and had refused all formal education once he left school. Alfonso had had a huge impact in those two short weeks.

They all met at a café in the centre of Malaga. It was an old fashioned café and had a history of attracting the more artistic, maverick, and fringe dweller types. Poets, musicians, story tellers and the general bohemians were completely at home there. They ate tapas and talked deeply, losing all track of time, wandering outside in the early evening to find the sun gone and their clothing inappropriate.

The café owner was a bohemian himself named Manalo. He had become good friends with Juan, a mutual admiration initiating the friendship, Juan appreciating his initiative and courage to set up a café unlike any other, and Manalo admiring Juan's passion for life and all things creative. The gift from Juan, a painting of the café hung proudly behind the counter, disappearing now and again between great billowing clouds of steam.

One afternoon Juan asked Manalo if he could advertise a weekly event to take place each Friday, where people could come and discuss and debate such things as music, art, poetry, freedom of speech, big brother, the removal of people's freedoms, the false flag of terrorism etc. A similar thing was happening already, true, but Juan wanted to organise and expand into something a bit more definite. Manalo was enthusiastic about the idea, not just for the extra custom it would bring.

"You have my permission and full blessing Juan; although I didn't know you were so interested in politics."

"I'm not really; I don't see it as political anymore. It's not important which side you think you are on, left, right or centre. Not even which culture you are from. You can call me left wing, right wing, anything, but the only wings that mean a thing are the ones that let you fly. The manifesto of new world order has no particular loyalty to any race, religion or belief. It wants to control, manipulate and terrorise you regardless of your skin colour or orientation. It is imperative that we do not let them divide us, that old trick they have used for thousands of years of divide and rule. So you see it is not political, it is more survival. We must come together and realise the enemy."

From these early discussions with Manalo a regular weekly event was indeed born. Juan named it "Coffee and Conspiracy," and he meticulously picked the various topics to discuss each week. They sat in small groups at the antique tables and then moved around to spread and share their observations and ideas. When most of the ideas were out and the discussion had peaked, Juan took centre stage and gave an impromptu overview.

Each topic was researched during the week and they brought their findings, facts, and opinions to the table. Juan made sure the micro chipping of the planet was regularly revisited as this outraged him a great deal. The spraying of chemicals from aeroplanes or chem trails as they are known came a close second. His research had confirmed what he had already noticed when he looked at the sky on a clear day and saw how the trails of vapour from the rear of passing aeroplanes that used to disappear in minutes, were actually staying around for hours, spreading from horizon to horizon and creating unusual looking skies.

Once more he turned to the internet in hope there may be some reference to this observation, and found a myriad of evidence which confirmed that we are being sprayed daily and world wide. Whether it's for weather modification, another assault on our immune system, or even a straight out de population strategy, it's a danger to us and we need to address it quickly, chemicals are falling on the crops we eat from, the reservoirs we drink from, and the land our children play on. The information is easy to obtain, the internet is a giant spanner in the works of the dark side and will assist mankind in its mass awakening. Don't turn a blind eye.

His research also guided him to the world of Orgonite or Orgone, a neutraliser of chem trails, tetra masts, and mobile phone masts, indeed the balancer of all the electro magnetic frequencies put out to harm you. He smiled in appreciation of the fact that the universe always has an answer.

The number of people attending grew by the week. Manalo's bank balance grew too. The café was perfectly situated for the university students who headed over there as soon as their Friday afternoon lectures had finished. Actually the Friday afternoon lessons became the least attended of the week, as people preferred the education of Juan's "Coffee and Conspiracy" to the regime of university teachings, so they usually sacrificed the lesson for an early start and a comfortable seat.

A healthy mixture of cultures and religions found their way there too, their youth and optimism brought forth the urgency to discuss and debate, to question, to seek justice. All of this they brought to a bustling café in Malaga, resistance and rebellion still thriving amongst the youth of Spain.

It is a fact that in Europe and America the new anti terror laws have made protest marches very difficult to make happen, coupled with the fact of most students are so heavily in debt through the necessity of having to obtain student loans and therefore work every spare hour they have just to survive, the energy of resistance has been suitably destroyed. The global elite do not leave a stone unturned in their totalitarian dream. Fortunately our rapidly growing awareness and elevating consciousness will not be found hiding under stones.

At the end of each session an action list was made and people volunteered for different tasks, contacting local councillors and politicians, mayors in town halls, advertising the forthcoming events and distributing information. The numbers were soon averaging a hundred, and Manalo, overworking his calculator, purchased an extra twenty sets of tables, chairs and umbrellas to utilise more outside space. He saw this as a good investment as the possibility that the growing numbers may otherwise seek bigger premises.

The topics were also expanding and matters of a more esoteric nature crept in. Meditation, healing, expanding consciousness, breath work, all found their way into the bubbling café. The more open and free willed they became the more powerful they felt. So instead of feeling overawed by these unseen powers, they actually began to see that apathy was not the only option available and the power lay in breaking out of the mass conditioning of thought form and re claiming the potential every human being has.

It was the same in each and every one of them, vastly different cultures realising that despite their obvious differences they wanted very similar things, and collectively they were finding ways of achieving it. Not by worrying about their differences but by focusing on what connected them.

Muslims, Christians, Catholics, Jews, Atheists, Hindus, and more in between were sending a message to local and eventually national media resources that there was no rift between them. And paradoxically, though most importantly, they found that the more they connected with each other in reality, the less they relied upon the scriptures of their chosen religions, to the point where a few of them even began to question the origins of them. To discover that they all derived from the same source and are a wonderful and intentional design to place people in mind prisons was a bit of an eye opener, I can tell you.

They discovered in the catharsis of that Malaga cafe that all religions work in exactly the same way. They impose a set of beliefs and idealisms and implement these through a code of conduct, rules and regulations which you then follow unquestioningly, and are then judged on being a good Catholic, Jew or whatever. This really is all it needs; the rest is self regulating and is run on the fuel of fear. But it was the fact that they all have the same origins which really blew those minds in there, sun, moon and serpent.

As Juan's friendships with the people from these different cultures deepened he began to mull over the reason of why there was seemingly so much reported hatred between the Muslims and those of the western societies. He asked his friends from North Africa how they felt about this and if they felt any deep routed anger or hatred towards him or other people from his culture. He asked friends from the Middle East the same thing and not one of them did, in fact they said they valued his friendship greatly and never actually thought about being any different from him.

Juan continued on this line of research (a dog with a juicy bone when our Juan is on to something) and asked his friends to see how their friends felt about relations between the two cultures, to see if the answers changed when they didn't know him personally. Exactly the same feeling came back to him. The overwhelming response was they had no reason to feel hatred towards anyone because of a perceived cultural difference.

Juan realised in a moment of absolute clarity that the world had been lulled into this idea of division and that it had been used for the advancement of an evil plan, a plan for total control. He thought about the fact that not too long ago Muslims and Christians, or Westerners and Easterners had no real conflict with each other, preferring just to get on with their lives and their beliefs quietly, while respecting everyone else's right to do the same. And in fact, despite the attempt to divide them, they still were. He instantly grasped the truth that nothing had actually changed between them because *they* were not at war. Suddenly the mist was clearing from the lake and he began to see what was at the bottom of it all.

There was no hatred between the vast majorities of these different people because it was just media propaganda for an agenda which ultimately aimed to control, manipulate and terrorise both sides indiscriminately, as its interests lay with nobody but themselves. The mantra of "Al Qaeda" had been used to mesmerise the watching world into a manufactured fear and hatred.

Juan's mind flashed back to Alfonso in the mountains and a time when he had spoke of "unseen forces of evil."

He had missed Alfonso from time to time but right now he felt it more than he had in ages. Once again one of Alfonso truths had set off a trigger deep inside of him, and Juan being Juan had no option but to fire the gun.

Back at his home, buzzing as he does, he thought about what he could do to put some positivism and light into the darkness of what was now glaringly obvious.

He went up to join his brothers and his mother and father on the rooftop, the October sunshine a perfect accompaniment as they entertained some friends with their music.

Juan picked up his guitar and played with a passion he'd been recently lacking. It felt good to be harmonising with the family once more.

When Juan's life took him through difficult periods and the peaks and troughs of self development wore him down, the family was an unchanging rock he could absolutely depend on.

The sun, squeezing out its last rays before the inevitable set, hit him square in the face. He pulled the sunglasses down from his head and relocated his hand immediately on neck of the guitar, correct chord found and business as usual. They each took turns at the main vocal, coming together whenever they felt like it to harmonise in thirds or fifths. They had been doing this from being very young and the skilful use of scales was completely natural for them. Two hours passed this way and the sun began its hurried descent behind the church, and in October that was like switching off the fire. One more song saw them heading down the blue iron stair case and into the warmth of the house, well, all but Juan. He reclined his chair, got comfy, stared up at the sky and watched the stars appearing one by one. He looked up into the infinity that is and reminded himself he is a spirit of the universe and not just the physical shell of an earthling.

Juan often explained this fact to people far more senior than himself, especially if they had the usual fear of death.

"You are of the universe," he would say. "If you are universal, why worry about leaving the world when it is a part of the universe anyway? Do you worry about leaving the kitchen to go to the living room in case you are not part of the house anymore?"

And what other people felt about his words he had no attachment to, for him it was an absolute truth.

He focused on slowing his breathing, the dogs, children, mothers and scooters did not disturb him from his focus anymore. He concentrated on his heart centre as he asked for direction and guidance. He thanked the universe for all the help it had given him up to now, and for all it will be giving him from now. This he did daily knowing gratitude is a precursor of even greater things to come. He would remain open and attentive for when the information did filter through.

The night grew darker still and the church informed the village it was eight o clock. Juan relaxed himself some more, shuffling bones into canvass, letting the darkness swallow him into sleep's inevitability. Within a minute he was dreaming, immaculate Japanese gardens with defined symmetry provided the exotic setting for his universal lesson. Towards the back of the garden was a gap between the perfectly cultivated bushes, a bright white expanse which slowly turned into a huge projector screen where he saw in giant letters the word ONENESS.

The letters faded away and were replaced with many images he had seen and experienced in his lifetime. He saw people waving banners for a socialist party. He saw people waving banners for a communist party. He then saw through the people and observed their souls desperately trying to connect with each other, souls crying at their separation from oneness.

Then there came people representing a left wing idealism and another set of people for the right wing. This disappeared and then came the determined face of the democrats and republicans. Once again this scene gave way and was replaced with one of Russian soldiers marching through streets and then one of American troops in their own uniforms, pride, passion, and hatred etched in their faces. The scenes were getting quicker and quicker, their duration shortening with each one until they were no more than flashes.

He saw a stadium with a hundred thousand people packed inside wearing two sets of colours and singing the most intense songs with an absolute passion that could not be matched in any other walk of life. And all for a bunch of men kicking a round ball up and down a piece of grass. He felt the hatred from each set of supporters, hating the men who wore different coloured shirts to theirs.

The Christians marching for Jesus felt they were more holy than Muslims praying to Allah, and they more holy than Buddhists praying to Buddha. They were all morphing in and out of the screen now. Black people against white people, rich against poor, famous against seemingly insignificant, even people from one district of a city feeling superior and separate to the people of another district, post code postulants tricked and duped beyond belief. He saw the strings and the attached puppeteers manufacturing the whole show; he noticed that they only looked half human, demonic entities playing humanity off against each other, divide and conquer perfectly executed.

The images were coming so fast now that he couldn't focus on one scene before it changed into another one. The colours got brighter and more vivid until eventually he had to look away.

When he looked back at the screen he saw in huge lilac letters the words . . .

KEEP YOUR CONNECTION TO THE SOURCE

The message rolled away to make way for another which read . . .

EACH OF US IS A UNIQUE SPARK OF THE SOURCE

Before Juan could digest this it changed once more to…

THE DEATH OF DIVISION IS THE BIRTH OF UNITY

Finally all the images reappeared in total chaos. The faces of the people looked tortured and contorted with pain. An ear piercing, whining noise accompanied the imagery, growing louder and louder until Juan thought he could stand no more. At the point of panic it abruptly ended and was replaced by one orchestrated note, f sharp for your jottings, bringing a balm to his suffering soul.

He looked at the screen and saw the spirit of every person rising upwards to meet in a huge white circle. The circle changed colour to an intense gold before he saw it fall apart and float above the gardens forming the words…

WE ARE ALL ONE

Juan woke and laughed at the simplicity of it all. He laughed also at the stupidity of it all and then wandered around the roof as free as a bird. The information was clear, break all boundaries, political leanings, religious preference, racial and cultural snobbery, flag waving in naive nationalism, put them all on the global back burner while we unite and get the job sorted.

Three days later he was back at the café bar organising a peace walk with as many of his friends as he could persuade. Not that they needed much persuading, they knew him, trusted him, and warmed to the idea instantly.

They had their various jobs to do, (very thorough old Delmore is) distributing leaflets, contacting media, thinking up slogans and making banners, the usual intricacies, essential nuts and bolts that allow the machine to take its glory.

He organised it to take place in a month, long enough for everyone to accomplish their individual and collective jobs and quick enough to satisfy Juan's impatience. The numbers doubled and doubled once more as one person asked ten people and ten people asked ten other people.

Juan was amazed at the response; his literature had obviously struck a chord in many people. He knew this was a powerful thing he was planning and the strength of it was in the fact that the message was coming from a peaceful, loving place. No anti government, no anti laws, in fact nothing anti at all, just pro peace, a simple show of unity from the so called opposing sides in a fabricated war. He had long since learned that peace could not be achieved by angry protest or violent means. The phrase "Peace by Peace" came to him and became the slogan for the march.

This was indeed the way forward for Juan as all they were doing was saying "we have no quarrel with each other, we know what you are up to and we stand together." With no protest, no violence and no anger, it is a very difficult situation for the authorities to deal with because they have no understanding of anything that comes from a dimension of love. They are almost trapped in another dimension that only operates through fear and hatred. Love is a world diametrically opposed to theirs. On a simpler level, it is impossible for them to arrest people when there is no action to react to.

Juan understood this in depth; his wisdom had expanded massively and allowed him the opportunity to see through the thin veils of so called reality. It was hard for him to convey this feeling in words, but he tried and was happy for the fact it was gathering momentum anyway.

By the time the march came the numbers had risen to around a thousand and included a few prominent speakers, respected poets and even a maverick politician. He just hoped there would be some journalists there who remembered they are here to serve the public and have the courage to tell it as it is, and not just the usual "tow the line" terrified types who plague the industry of journalism.

They met at the square in front of the cathedral in the centre of Malaga. The route had been carefully planned after the necessary permission from the authorities to conduct the walk had been obtained, a feat still possible for you at the moment. Just.

Careful planning had ensured that the local news channels had been informed and would at least be there to witness the event on camera. It even made it onto one national news channel, which considering it is also ultimately controlled by these forces was a great achievement.

Many newspapers also covered the story and the first "Peace by Peace" walk had been a total success.

One man with one simple idea had organised and executed all of that because he cared for the future of his world. He could not sit back and allow what was being planned to take place, and if the plans of a total take over and a micro chipped world was successful, at least he would be able to look people in the eye and say, "I tried, what did you do?"

34

KEEPING LIGHT

If your body is a container what are you filling it with? What thoughts are you putting in your mind? Take time to fill it with light and positivism. Breathe in deeply and fully and breathe out all of the garbage.

Three months passed and Juan had heard nothing from Hacham, then on an afternoon of rare rain, he casually took the call that would assassinate his current life style.

"Good news for you Juan," he had said on the telephone, unable to stifle his excitement. "We have got an exhibition in morocco. It's in three weeks time, can you make it?"

Juan could make it of course; a diary with nothing much in, confirmed it as a definite. Arrangements were carefully made and in those three weeks he threw himself into the world of painting. Not that he needed to do any for the exhibition; the paintings had already been selected and placed in beautiful frames, chosen and purchased by Hacham, frames that had cost more than Juan had ever earned with his art, but he just wanted to absorb himself in the passion of his work so he was in the right zone for the exhibition.

In three weeks he had completed four new paintings. His favourite one he gave the name "What difference?" and it ended up becoming the image used to promote future "Peace by Peace" events.

When Hacham stood back and looked at the collection of twenty wonderful paintings, temporarily hanging in his own gallery room, he saw them in the light necessary to appreciate the obvious quality they possessed. Frames always enhance a painting, but it was more than just that. When they were all together, displayed in the same way he had seen thousands of others displayed, he could almost see the soul of the artist. He could see the individuality of each picture but he could also see the overall style of the artist, a style that was screaming its uniqueness.

Juan's mum and dad were asking many more questions than Juan was used to. They had always given him a virtual free hand to play, even though they weren't always sure what he was striving for. But with the "Peace by Peace" growing so rapidly and now this exhibition in Tangiers, it suddenly hit them their own child was becoming quite a legend.

Some of their recent questioning however left Juan a little uncomfortable. It was one thing to discuss these universal matters amongst like minded friends, but however much he was a campaigner for truth, he didn't like being the one who had to show them the world they thought they knew was a million miles away from reality.

"The end is not written yet," he assured them. "I have to write my pages positively and trust that everything will turn out the right way. No-one knows how the scales are balanced. We have to think powerfully. Every thought produces energetic vibrations, we don't see them of course but the air is full of who we are. We are never shown what people really believe about the way the world is controlled so we don't know the actual number of the people who are rapidly waking up. We only see the propaganda version on our televisions and in our newspapers. I think if everyone can do a small thing each day towards waking people up to what is happening in the world their children will have to live in one day, and also the world we ourselves will return to, we will tip those scales from dark to light. Drip by drip till it tips. That's why I don't get despondent, because I don't know how the scales are balanced. It could be the smallest action that sees them tip. The mass consciousness of the planet would then change and we would create a place to be proud of. There is a light pouring on to the planet at this time. It's as though we have all been coded somehow to wake up at this point, astrologically, scientifically, and historically we are living in a very powerful time."

His mum and dad nodded in agreement but like most parents they only wished their son would get a proper job.

35

EXHIBITIONS

Imagine all of your actions, your thoughts, your words and intentions were hung in a gallery. Would anyone pay to see them?

Juan woke on a crisp November morning to another clear blue sky. November in southern Spain still produces warm sunny days, the cold and damp being kept out by a domineering sun, well at least until January and February when it gave winter its small consolation prize.

Hacham had arranged to collect Juan late afternoon, providing his ferry crossing sailed on time and the custom officers were feeling more benevolent than awkward, and don't, as they so often do, make the mistake of thinking that power comes from a well pressed uniform.

Juan would be staying for five days, with the exhibition beginning on the fourth day, he had no idea what to expect either from the exhibition or the stay at Hacham's family home.

He packed a few things in an old rucksack and then climbed up the steps to his rooftop. Leaning on the perimeter wall and looking downwards to the village, as he had done a thousand times before, he reflected on how his life had unfolded since that meeting with Alfonso. He had always wanted to go back to Methina Fondales and see him again, but something had always got in the way to prevent it happening. Now the picture he had rushed so nervously to Aljibe as a boy had reconnected him with Alfonso. He wondered how Alfonso would feel if he did track him down again. Maybe he had done all he needed to do with him anyway, he inadequately convinced himself.

Juan stared down at the houses below him, contemplating on all those people and all those lives. He thought about the way they lived, behind those walls and doors, in completely different worlds to his own, living the lives of doctors, drivers, shepherds, housewives, shopkeepers, school children, alcoholics, thieves and holy men, and alcoholic, thieving holy men, all in the same village but in very different worlds.

He smiled at the nature of his thoughts, shook his head and wandered around his rooftop, making full use of the 360 degree views. There were mountains to the rear, the village to the front, other family rooftops to one side, and the very back of the village with the road out to Sayalonga on the last side. He was blessed with a view for all moods.

"Juan, come down for lunch," his mother shouted, preparing enough food for the full five days he was away.

"I can't eat all that," he laughed, seeing the banquet she had made half covering the dining table.

"Well you don't know about their food there, its Africa you know."

"Yes I know mum, and if they try to serve me trunk of elephant, I shall be on the first camel home."

Mum ignored the comment and stood by the table pointing to his favourite bits, enticing him to at least begin.

He passed an hour away dutifully eating what he could before nipping across the street to tell his good friend Roberto he was about to leave for the exhibition.

Roberto and Juan had grown up in the village together, gone to the same school and shared their hopes and dreams. The only difference between them now was that Juan was still following his dreams while Roberto had allowed life to crush his.

"Good luck Juan, come back a rich man and I will serve your every need my master."

Juan held him tightly with the closeness and comfort that years of baring souls and sharing goals had brought.

Hacham had docked at Algejeras and was already heading out of the port. He had chosen his Mercedes E Class for the trip. He would average a speed 100 M.P.H. plus, which would see him at the house in little over one and a half hours.

He telephoned Juan to let him know he was on his way. The call was confirmation for Juan that he was really going to Morocco in Africa where his paintings were going on display in an art gallery. His excitement intensified and he tried numerous tricks to move time forward to Hacham's arrival, failing hopelessly on every account. It was his mum who rescued him from the cruelty of the clock by listing items for unlikely eventualities which had him panicking and squashing more things into a now bulging rucksack. In the middle of his panic came the knock on the door.

Hacham had come alone. Juan's mother who had suddenly had a change of clothing appeared with a housewife elegance whipped up in seconds, welcomed him into their home.

"Hello Mrs Santiago," Hacham beamed. "It's wonderful to see you both again. Tell me, where is your husband?"

"He is working today, couldn't get time off. My daughter is somewhere though," she said, already heading to the back of the house to look for Alba. Normally she would have yelled from whatever location she was at, even if Alba was playing down the street. Decorum however was maintained that day and she returned with her pretty daughter and more introductions were made.

"Come and have a drink and some food before you set off back, I can't believe you've come all the way from Africa and are going straight back there."

She said the word Africa again with no awareness of north and south. Even after Juan had explained how close they were in miles she still said, "yes but Africa."

Hacham was lead by the elbow to the table where the food was left over after Juan's brave attempt at eating five days worth. He politely struggled to make the banquet smaller, but despite he and Juan both eating till they could no more, the amount of food on the table barely changed. They ate more than they wanted, hugged, and waved goodbye within forty five minutes.

Another forty five minutes saw them passing through Malaga, heading to the outskirts of Marbella. The Mercedes and the quiet motorway with the surface like glass got on very well and tongues loosened as the miles were eaten up.

They discussed the upcoming exhibition and Hacham tried to explain to Juan in his basic Spanish about the protocol and what he should expect.

"This could really earn you a lot of money you know Juan. I have priced each painting for you, but only if you agree of course. It is your work and you own it. I just did this to save time. There will be many people attending the exhibition and many experts in the field. If you wanted it there is the opportunity also to do some interviews for magazines and newspapers which will give you more exposure, if it suits you of course. I personally think the art world will be raving about your work."

Juan tried to stay cool as though this happened all the time. He was more excited about the exposure it would bring him than the adulation and had already been thinking of ways in which he would use any fame it brought to help wake the planet up to what was really happening to its sleepy inhabitants. By the time they pulled in at the manic port of Algejeras he had already worked out how he would accomplish this.

The crossing was quick and uneventful and a calm November sea made Juan's first ever sail out of Spain a pleasurable one. He and Hacham were standing on the deck as the boat negotiated its parking spot at Cueta.

Juan was surveying the buildings in the distance, forcing himself on African landscape. He took some deep breaths to accentuate his experience. Hacham was enjoying watching Juan and his idiosyncratic ways. He had a lot of questions stored for when they relaxed their egos and greased the gates of language.

"Well Juan, we should be home in under an hour."

"Wow, I can't wait. It all looks incredible already."

"Yes it's so close to Spain, and even though we do share some architectural similarities through the Muslim and Christian occupations of our respective countries, you are going to know for sure you are in a different continent."

Hacham's comments were soon validated as they slowly crossed the check point between the two countries. Cueta, even though on Moroccan soil still belongs to Spain. However the streams of Moroccan traders marching up and down with the welfare of their families strapped to their backs, carried on their heads, pushed in decrepit wheelchairs, or packed onto old bicycles which were pushed not ridden, diluted the technicalities of Spanish ownership.

The whole of the border was a huge mobile market and sent a rush of excitement through Juan's veins.

"Thank you so much for this opportunity, I don't know if another one would have come along so easily for me. I have done nothing but paint a few pictures."

"It gives me great pleasure to watch a brand new artist emerge and also see how the art world reacts to them. It's what makes me tick Juan, and I have a very good feeling about your work."

36

TEMPTATION

No lesson on earth can be more powerful than one which alights every emotion. But in truth it is still an illusion.

Jack and Florence were travelling also. They had done their share of behind the scenes organising along with Soran and were just as excited as Hacham and Juan at the fortunes of his progress. They joined him, subtle as a breeze in a gale, as he spent time with Falak and Latif, wishing only that Annabelle and Colleen could be there for the impromptu re union, but density is a difficult state to influence and it would have to wait a while longer.

Colleen was already nine years old; inquisitive, bordering bossy; she had a big influence on most matters at home. Annabelle and Eammon were amazed at her ability to subtly manipulate events. They were still living in the cottage as the owners had stayed abroad much longer than anticipated, hinting that when they did finally return, they were almost certain that they would base themselves in London and were happy for them to continue renting the cottage for the foreseeable future.

Annabelle's mum had finally moved in with them due to failing health. She had rented out the house where she had spent so many happy years with Roy, a move which upset her greatly even though she would be with her family and receiving their much needed input.

Annabelle had had a hard time since the death of her father. It was difficult caring for Colleen and her mother, fortunately, in one respect at least; she had been able to give up her part time job at a local café due to the fact that Eammon was constantly busy and earning enough for them all to be comfortable. His sufficient income coupled with the low rental of the cottage and the contribution from her mum, made them as financially comfortable as they had ever been.

She was sad to leave her work in another way though. Here's why. In the last few months she had grown close to a young colleague who had come to work at the happy café. He came from the town of Westport and was staying with his auntie in Mulranny after finishing a degree in psychology at Dublin University. The two of them had connected instantly, Annabelle still carrying her obvious pain, and James with his fresh from university philosophy and bounding enthusiasm for all he encountered were a natural synergistic blend.

Working had become something to look forward to as their wavelengths merged and her usual shyness buckled and eventually collapsed.

Annabelle and her vast local knowledge was able to indulge James in the greatest visual delights of Mulranny, a happy historian eager to please, and if their shift finished at the same time, as it often did, through undetected manipulation of the rota, they would head off to a place of natural beauty or interest

James drove a 1972 Vauxhall Viva which Annabelle adored. It had that old smell of worn leather and acquired musk which transported them both back to an era in which neither had played a part in. This blue iconic work of art was a great conversation starter too, creating attention, defusing tension, and working like a magnet to the young and old alike. It had made him many acquaintances in the short time he had been there, unable to park the car without a friendly head popping through the open window for a sniff down memory lane.

He spoke with a fierce passion for the 1960s and 1970s fashions, designs and ethos. Not quite brave enough to wear any of its outrageous offerings, he did have a style of his own which definitely borrowed some core elements from those periods of time where designing and architecture actually meant something to someone.

He felt a yearning to be a part of that freedom and the hope that seemed to radiate from the pores of everyone on the planet at that time. He told Annabelle it was mostly due to the music of the Beatles, opening the minds of the sleeping masses in just five years, from simple love songs through to the mind expanding experience that was Sergeant Pepper.

"The doors of the inquisitive and rebellious were first booted open by the timely arrival of Elvis Pressley who raised the bar from tepid to fever pitch," he told an enthused Annabelle. "The Beatles then casually strolled through it and with the combined forces of the lyrical genius of the likes of Bob Dylan, Donovan, The Byrds and The Kinks amongst many more; the planet had great reason to feel hopeful and free. And indeed it did feel free. Who would have guessed back then how tepid the general music scene would become and how enslaved, brainwashed, and dumbed down the majority of that generation's children would end up?

We need another musical explosion, something with all the ingredients of love, freedom, hope and determination to change our destiny before this system finally nails us to the straight and narrow. Something with the impact of Punk rock but the idealism of hippy philosophy, and maybe without the drugs," he informed Annabelle one afternoon as they cruised towards Westport. "The drugs were of course a great part in the expansion of human consciousness and a wonderful conveyor of love, but a terrible hindrance when it came to the necessary organisation of revolution. It was a very close thing however," he added in regretful tones. "A close thing indeed."

Westport was home for James and he was taking her for a brief tour of his hometown and the prestigious Westport house where the great Grace O Malley had once resided. Annabelle's great, great, great, great, great Grandma she told him jokingly. (Same sir name you see.)

As they exited the car James carried on with his version of events surrounding the redeeming qualities of musical revolution.

"Annabelle," he said, holding the outsides of her shoulders to emphasise the profundity. "I can't understand why the great rock and roll bands of our time haven't realised what is going on regarding the removal of our personal freedoms and ever increasing surveillance of our every move. They could get together and perform a mammoth concert to raise awareness and demand its immediate demise. Music is the strongest medium to do it, and what's more it could be instant. The powers must be laughing hysterically at this missed opportunity.

I know we have had the "feed the world" type things, and as good as its intention was, they never addressed the problem of the ruling elite. Nothing was exposed so nothing ever really changed. I thought rock music was meant to be challenging and thought provoking?"

"Yes I agree with that," Annabelle said, who was new to all this information but was sufficiently inspired by words that effortlessly rolled off his tongue.

"Imagine the power of a stadium full of people with open minds and open hearts, as the band whose music they love performed there. There is a type of euphoria and a high level energy exchange in those situations anyway, anything is possible."

He let go of her shoulders and settled for a gesticulated lecture.

"Our greatest artists playing one concert, televised all around the world and informing the world of what is going on and to wake up to it, then switching to the right brain with their music and allowing it to be absorbed into people's consciousness, well that would be something really worth doing, providing the lyrical content was adapted too."

"Such passionate words from one so young," Annabelle teased.

"Seriously Annabelle, we need more like Patti Smith and Neil Young, Bob Dylan did it too, to an extent, but people with the courage to stand by their principles, that's what I'm talking about, to deliver a clear message and do all they can to make a difference, true legends in my book. I'm sure there must be others too, but nowhere near enough. Neil Young actually released a song called "Impeach the president," you can't get clearer than that can you?"

"Muse," Annabelle shouted, much louder than she wanted.

"Muse? James repeated. "On what?"

"Muse, the band, the song, Uprising, you know it don't you? It talks about opening the third eye, and not being scared of dying. We will be victorious, course you know it. They must be on it mustn't they?"

"Yes you're right, they must be. I forgot about them. Maybe something will occur after all."

"Well, maybe you can be the one to organise it when your band becomes successful," she smiled.

James' band was an eclectic mix of influences which ranged from psychedelic sixties through to country and folk, and yet somehow they managed to fuse it into a style of their own. James played guitar and offered his lid lifting lyrics to the songs. After the summer they planned to get back together and have a serious attempt at infiltrating the music industry. James thought often about having an opportunity to put his ideas to use and hoped he could go that far.

In the weeks they had worked together, the two of them had become the most talked about couple in county Mayo, or so it had felt like to Annabelle. The usual "were they or weren't they" debate seemed to offer much more spice than the "Soup of the day."

Annabelle wasn't happy with the gossip, she didn't need that kind of attention reaching Eammon, even though she knew she did harbour some unexamined feelings which although well buried, still sat uncomfortably inside her.

James on the other hand had nothing to lose. He felt good around her and made no secret of the fact. He constantly complimented her on her looks and her personality and did it with such genuineness it was impossible to refute, teasing her shiny black hair into different styles, roughing it up and then starting all over again. He was a man unperturbed by the danger of his own actions.

Eammon and James were not similar; in fact they had completely different personalities. James was comfortable sharing his opinions and passions to anyone who would listen, while Eammon, in the main, gave little away. Most of the conversations between him and Annabelle had become increasingly superficial, not that she minded too much, the love was still shown, from both sides, but sometimes she wished they had more depth to their relationship which would allow her to understand him and his feelings better. All their conversations seemed to be based around work, Annabelle's mother, the house or Colleen. She missed the times when they used to share their hopes and dreams and feelings for each other, an intimacy which was now certainly being fulfilled by James.

Even when her friendship with James developed more and Eammon saw a happier Annabelle emerging, he said nothing and asked no questions. He did however suddenly find an influx of new work and told her she no longer needed to earn and could concentrate on looking after her mother more. Annabelle suspected insecurity there but didn't bother to ask as she already knew the lid would be firmly screwed down on the jar of jealousy.

So, as much as she loved her job in the little café, her life had in fact become a balancing act and she felt relieved that at least she was retiring from the frustration of her plate spinning life style.

Her last shift had been a mournful affair, with a feeling of inevitable doom around the café. Conversation laboured between her and James as the morning marched on unswervingly.

"What time do you have to be home today?" he asked casually at the cream cake trolley.

"I have a couple of hours to spare if you want to go somewhere."

"What about the beach at Mulranny? I don't think I'll be able to go after today. It won't be the same without you."

"I'm sure it would be," she said, refusing to accept the fact he may be right. "I'll pop in at home first if that's alright, best check on mum you know."

Lightness once more filled the café, one simple arrangement lifting the gloom by extending their friendship by two hours or so.

37

MORALITY

Morals are another set of rules, man made for the minds of the weak. Right and wrong is a knowing in the heart.

They parked the Vauxhall and weaved their way down to the beach. At the small drop where the path runs out, the routine hand was offered from James and accepted graciously, instinctively to be dropped between their third and fifth step. An agreement had been sub consciously made that a hand held beyond five steps implied frivolity more than chivalry. Today they broke the routine and with it the unwritten rules.

After around ten steps there was a sideward glance from Annabelle, an apologetic smile from James and a statement of intent by a firmer squeeze of their hands.

They walked in silence until they reached the rock, their individual internal dialogue reaching a crescendo. They sat down, hands now clasped, and outward conversation muted. James spoke first, surprising himself with his instantaneous observation.

"I think I am going to leave the café, I didn't know till just now but working there has been more about being with you than serving pots of tea. It's probably time for me to go back home and make a start on my life. Thanks for making me welcome here, but I'll be honest with you, I wouldn't have stayed this long if I had been working with just Ethel, Rose, and Mrs O Donnell."

Annabelle pushed a small rock back and forth with her foot, a meaningless task going nowhere, the perfect outward display as she searched to find meaning in her now fragile friendship.

"I wonder why we did meet each other at this time in our lives," she asked, still rock rolling.

"We won't ever know that will we Annabelle?"

"Is this the end of it do you think, or will we see each other again?" she said, immediately cursing the death sentence she had risked.

"I don't know Annabelle, I will be visiting my Auntie now and again, I could come and see you, if it didn't cause too much trouble."

Each statement seemed such a lifeless and futile offering in comparison to the life force that had previously imbued their friendship. The words felt like rocks being thrown off a cliff.

They stared in silence across to the sea and shared in its cold, dead emotion. When James looked at Annabelle he saw the tear gently leaving the corner of her eye and beginning its journey down the face. He held her face in his hands and wiped the tear with his thumb. Then her head was guided onto his shoulder and the arms placed around her slight frame before they finished the move with a meaningful hug. Neither knew how long a hug was allowed, the rules were vague, the laws were unmade, and the experience was being written in the moment.

If it was their last meeting then they had to cram maybe fifty years of loving each other, a few children and grandchildren raised, a few hundred holidays, thousands of meals shared, and the till death us do part commitment into five minutes. And if parallel lives are possible they are living one right now.

In their Earth dimension however, they managed one more hug outside her home before she closed the door on the Vauxhall Viva and unknowingly on the friendship, that final clunk of the heavy door condemning all their feelings to memory.

Annabelle walked through the gate of the cottage, through the front door and into the comforting arms of normality. It felt good for a short while, no monumental decisions to make and the clarity of routine was momentarily welcome.

She hid the crumpled café receipt with James's phone number scrawled on the back in a bedroom drawer before going into the kitchen, switching on the oven and preparing tea for Eammon, hoping the routine ritual would carry a secret healing.

She felt Eammon's presence behind her and turned to greet him. The shock of no-one being there only lasted a second, it had happened many times before and Annabelle was certain it was her father, somehow being around when she needed comfort or strength.

He was of course there many times, watching events from a gap in the fabric of time. There was usually some evidence left behind, the fire roaring when she returned to the room, knowing she had left it smouldering, the smell of wood smoke wafting past at random moments, the darting shadows in the corners of her awareness were all evidence that her father had been visiting. She said nothing to no-one about her suspicion of these spirit visits.

I have to say, from my privileged position here, my complimentary seat in the grand stand, access all areas if you don't mind, Annabelle was quietly achieving her challenge of giving unconditionally and without expecting anything in return. Her relationship with Colleen was a very loving one and although it was early days, it looked as though perhaps they would achieve the harmony in this incarnation they had hoped for. Yet in this snippet of a troubled timeframe she was experiencing, this molecule of emotional existence, achieving a cosmic challenge meant little to her.

It was the fifth day after her departure from the café, after dropping off Colleen at school, the heavy heart and the drained spirit gave up. She had tried to delete him from her thoughts but James was camping in her head. As she approached the café she was completely oblivious to everything around her. She marched onwards robotically, mentally visualising the hug which would resuscitate her dead body. She no longer cared what anyone thought. Through the door she went, oblivious to her ex colleague's looks of surprise, expertly negotiating the obstacle course of tables and chairs before braking hard in the kitchen area.

"Is James in?" she casually asked the manageress.

"No he's not Annabelle. I thought you would have known. He went back home, never even gave us a chance to replace him. Have you come back to help us out?"

Annabelle didn't hear the last few words. She had already turned and was retracing her course through the café.

She was back on the street before taking the luxury of a full breath, waiting five full minutes before stepping on the on time bus. People were talking to the driver about the possibility of putting up a shelter at their bus stop as it was always windy there, someone else in ear shot was commenting on the unsualness of the low tide, and Annabelle, blending in as best she could was drowning in the tide of triviality.

Back on her bed at home she sunk into the pillows and surrendered herself to her fate. She felt numbness and hyper sensitivity trading places by the second and she snarled at the Gods and their absence of intervention.

Entering the lounge she saw her mother and instantly resented her for needing help transferring from the wheelchair. She engaged herself in the task but not in conversation. To the kitchen now, she unscrewed the top off a bottle of wine and took a good long swig. She checked the clock, 10 a.m. the red digits flashed, emphasising the a.m. in their own neon way. Back upstairs and on the bed, she emptied most of the bottle of wine in less than fifteen minutes while reflecting on the possibilities of her whole life being spent dwelling on the fringes and swinging on the hinges of a love unknown.

She gazed around the bedroom, at the photographs in their frames, mum and dad, Eammon and Colleen, the one from their holiday in the Lakes, the present of the porcelain couple embracing that Eammon had bought for her. She tried to force her feelings for him, trick her spirit with logic and come out victorious.

The wine gave her a physical explanation for the numbness she now felt. Within ten minutes she was fast asleep.

Up here none of this is important.
You will not even remember its triviality.
There are no words in this head that doesn't exist to express the sheer beauty of the golden ecstasy that you will encounter when you cross over.

It doesn't even matter which path you take as your world is only a dream.
Take the easy path with Eammon, like a stroll on a summer day.
Take the changing path with James where you develop courage to face the people you leave behind.
Take another path altogether, one of mudslides and quicksand where you arrive filthy and exhausted.
It matters not as they all go up the same mountain and finish at the golden peak.
Different routes up a mountain of dreams where thought is the compass.
Don't waste a moment dwelling over the wrong path. There is NO SUCH THING.
Set your compass and go without fear or indecision.
You have already agreed all the situations and events you find yourself in.
My love, I wish you could see things from this vantage point, where the mind and body disappear and all that's left is love and light.
There is a wonderful opportunity for you to be in the world and bask in its rich abundance.
Enjoy every aspect by being true to yourself and only doing what your heart believes in.
You have nothing to lose as you will end up here no matter what.
You will regret indecision far more than you will regret wrong decision.
Like a tree in the wind learn how to bend, as the rigid tree will snap.
Each minute you waste has gone for good, so seize the opportunity.
If you wake tomorrow and Eammon has left you, you will be heartbroken for a different reason.
It is only your thinking that is broken, not your heart.
I am with you every moment.
Your loving Dad.

She woke up in utter confusion, still drunk from the wine, no idea of time, and wondering if the note she had just read was real. She remembered it had been left on the mantelpiece where dad always used to leave his notes. She ran to the fireplace but it wasn't there. She hazily remembered hiding something in the bedroom drawer and stumbled her way there only to realise it was the crumpled café receipt as a bit more memory returned.

She sat on the edge of the bed, little by little the pieces began to fit together and she realised that the note had been nothing more than a dream. She wondered how it could have been possible, the words had been so clear, she could even remember some of them although they were fading quickly.

Annabelle crept back downstairs and saw her mum asleep on her chair. She stood and stared at the ailing body, slowly lifting her gaze to the story book of the face. The deepened lines of grief, the heavy, sunken eyes of sadness, sallow skin where vibrancy once was. The story left her with an overwhelming feeling of love and compassion.

When Margaret awoke, her daughter's head was in her lap. She immediately began stroking her face and hair as she had done since the day she was born. A lifelong commitment unquestioningly carried out.

"You will be alright sweet; you know life is never too easy. But even the worst imaginable pain fades in time."

Annabelle wondered how much her mum knew about James, the way she always wondered how she knew things.

Neither one mentioned the dichotomy; Margaret because it wasn't important for her to know, just to be there for Annabelle, and Annabelle not sure if her mum did know or not, so saw no point in risking unnecessary disclosure.

They stayed there for ten minutes, crying out their separate sadness. Annabelle broke away first. "Let's do what dad would have done in this situation and make some tea."

"Yes he would have for sure, always the kettle for a crisis."

"Do you still miss him mum?" she chanced while the communication door was open.

"All the time. I still feel him around now and again you know, though I know it's probably an over imaginative mind longing for it to be true."

"No I think it too; sometimes I just know he has been here."

She never mentioned the dream. She had to work it all out first and wait until she could file it away in a compartment she understood. She felt a whole lot better by the time Eammon came home from work and nothing was ever mentioned about the events of that uneasy day.

38

TRAVEL

Every mile travelled on foreign soil opens the mind by the same degree.

Juan's senses were on high alert as they entered Morocco, eyes loading visual treats and storing them in the brain/mind for the future, ears straining for new sounds and frequencies, nose twitching as the olfactory system made its first diagnosis of Morocco.

Juan said he was surprised how green it was, and then laughed with Hacham as to why he thought it would be any different.

As they headed towards Tetouan, it rose majestically to greet them, posing on top of the slope, rising from a huge valley with the massive dark rock behind it.

"This dramatic setting of the sombre Rif Mountains and the bright and colourful Martil valley is what gives it its enchanting and surreal quality. From its faded white walls you will see uninvited, demonstrative colours, and the green tiled roofs nicely topping off the mixture of Spanish and Moorish styling."

Juan's first history lesson had begun.

"The town itself was established in 1305. Later it became a pirate's lair before being destroyed in the fifteenth century. It was rebuilt by Andalusian refugees of both Jewish and Muslim origin, carrying forward the charm and sophistication of Moorish Andalusia. You can still see the tradition of aristocracy in the medina architecture; the houses in Tetouan have more of a feel of the old Arab quarters found in such cities as your own country's Cordoba, Cadiz or Seville.

Look Juan, see how tall and square the houses are with their iron balconies and ornately decorated windows. Tetouan in Berber means "open your eyes" and is believed to be a reference to its hap hazard construction," he told him, stopping briefly for breath and reflection.

They moved on through the city centre of crowded streets and lively souks, Juan becoming more animated by the second. He saw massive diversity in the style of clothing worn and was confused as to the origin of anyone.

Women on street corners were selling honey, butter, vegetables and herbs in their strangely mixed clothing. Further on he saw a group of girls leaving a building and couldn't stop himself asking, "Where are those girls from?"

"They are college students finishing for the day, are you curious about their different styles?"

"Well yes, some look Spanish and others, well, classic African I suppose."

"You will find a great mixture here Juan, even amongst the local girls there will be huge contrast of fashion depending on their belief system. It's a multi faceted fashion parade."

Indeed two of the girls did have full Muslim dress, including the Hijab, others were wearing jeans and T shirts with a definite European look. Two more had flamboyant dresses, more typical of the style from the west coast of Africa. Juan liked Morocco.

They drove through the bustle of the city centre and then down a huge road lined with trees toward the outskirts before reaching a small hamlet of houses where Hacham stopped and pointed out his own dwelling.

"Which one?" Juan asked, pointing at what looked like three or four houses together.

"It's all that building, it is one house Juan."

Juan laughed, shaking his head in disbelief as he took stock of the huge fronted mansion with an enormous driveway and gated entrance.

Hacham clicked a key fob and the imposing iron gates swung open. He looked at Juan, enjoying his array of expressions and obvious delight.

"Come on, let's go inside," he said, guiding him with parental tenderness.

They walked through the double fronted door and into a spectacular courtyard, housing an illuminated swimming pool. Small lanterns with candles inside flanked the four sides of the pool. The floor was tiled in a natural stone colour, only a shade different to the colour of the twenty metre walls which formed the courtyard. Nestled into one of the walls, the one opposite the entrance was an alcove with an up lighter in each corner and two huge bundles of candles which had been lit as a welcome for Juan. Two wicker tables with white table cloths and candles completed this surreal scene, mesmerising Juan as the alcove flashed and flickered its orange welcome.

He looked up, casually noting the numerous rooms leading off two, three sided balconies, one directly above the other. His busy eyes were struggling to keep up with his demanding senses. He had never even left the boundaries of Spain before, never crossed those lines of make believe division, never tip toed through those fabricated fences of divide and rule, and now here he was, dwelling in a palace of such obvious wealth and stature, an outstanding moment in Juan's life, undoubtedly. Through another door and they were in the grand lounge, paintings hung with sporadic brilliance, vying for attention.

The huge floor, on which sat probably Morocco's finest tiles and worthy of being displayed themselves, were six huge Persian rugs, placed with the obvious intention of achieving a geometric treat.

Hacham walked to the bottom of the grand staircase and shouted his wife and children. Juan heard the names Zahra, Latif and Falak being called and the following Arabic conversation reinforced the fact he was on foreign territory, an observation which left him with closed eyes and a smug smile.

Falak was first to come down the stairs, bounding her way over she embraced Juan with an openness which suggested their friendship was far greater than just the one short meeting. Juan felt a closeness which took him by surprise, off guard and slightly shocked, he broke the embrace hastily.

She was dressed in dark blue jeans and white woollen jumper, her long black hair was untied and fell down past her shoulders. Juan did not notice her beauty when they had visited him in Spain. He noticed now. A firm handshake and a well rehearsed two cheek kiss followed from Latif and Zahra.

Within ten minutes the honoured guest was eating cake and enthusiastically sipping his first cup of mint tea, attentively swallowing down the culture.

"We need to take your pictures to the gallery tomorrow. We can sort them out later on, if you're not too tired of course."

Hacham was just as excited at taking Juan into his own gallery, the thought of his reaction on seeing his paintings all hung and framed had been constantly drip feeding his merriment. Juan of course, didn't even know they had been framed. He hadn't thought about anything like that.

When the tea and ice break cake was finished, Hacham led them up three sets of stairs and out onto the rooftop, spectacular views across the whole of Tetouan and over to the Rif Mountains on offer. The patio which facilitated this incredible vista was immense. At one side there was a six foot high wall running right across the terrace, it was part of an adjoining outbuilding and had been utilised to form the backdrop of the shaded area. All along the wall were huge cushions pushed together, with a larger one on each end, triumphantly creating a giant chaise lounge. The whole thing was covered in a cream Hessian material with around twenty scatter cushions for backrests. Four rugged wooden poles had been set into the concrete at each corner, and fastened to the poles with rope hung giant canvas sheets to provide the essential shade. To finish off this meticulously designed rooftop, a large red carpet had been placed in front of the seats. It housed three low, dark wood tables; each one displaying a large antique lantern placed accurately in the centre. The whole effect was stunning and caused Juan to momentarily think about his rooftop at home and how, if he earned enough money, he would treat his mum and dad to something similar, well similar in style if not size.

They sat for a while, sharing stories and bringing their lives so far up to date. You know that feeling don't you? The one where everything is new and layered with anticipation. I said you would didn't I? Anyway, they asked him lots of questions which naturally evolved into Alfonso and their meeting in the mountains.

"I can't believe you haven't seen him since then Juan. Wouldn't you like to?"

"Yes, of course I would love to, I'm certain I will return one day. I'm just never sure how he would respond. He's brilliant but unpredictable."

The sun was dipping behind the mountains and the lights in Tetouan were responding accordingly. One by one they played their tiny part until the whole city was illuminated.

Juan was reluctant to move. He felt privileged to be sharing this evening, this setting and this endearing warmth from his new friends.

"Come on young man," Hacham eventually said. "We'll go and sort out your paintings before we come back to the terrace for the evening meal."

He led the way followed by Juan, Zahra, and then Falak and Latif close behind.

Back down the stairs they went, to the top balcony, through a door a couple of centuries old, and then down a corridor into a huge open room, with Juan, naturally thrilled but wondering why he was being followed so closely.

"Step inside Juan," Hacham told him, satisfied with his clever concealment.

As he entered, he switched the light on, purposefully positioned for maximum effect and they all stared expectantly at Juan, waiting for his predictable reaction.

"Well what do you think?"

Juan looked around the huge room with no reaction. It was obvious he hadn't recognised his own work yet. He walked over to the nearest painting and stared at it for long enough to cause concern from his audience.

"It's mine," he finally shouted, taking a few steps back, tilting his head and re examining his work. He then raced from one picture to the next with his jaw dropped and eyes like two dinner plates. It took him a full five minutes to finish viewing his own exhibition. Then speechless he walked over to Hacham and hugged him, no words necessary. As they let go of their embrace Falak threw her arms around him while mum patted his back and Latif placed his hands on his shoulders.

After this spontaneous mobbing Juan said, "thank you all so much, I really had no idea. So much trouble you must have gone to. I cannot believe how good they look, I mean how different."

He walked around them all again while the family spoke in Arabic about joy, contentment and other similar things.

The evening got even better for Juan; a wonderful meal looking out over the city lights, two bottles of red wine shared, more stories exchanged, minor confessions and a general warmth which pervaded the whole affair made it a surreal first night.

Juan could not compare with the great tales of travel they had collected. He did however captivate them with his theories and maverick ideas. They liked him more and more as the wine helped to unfold his character. Music became a topic late on and he confessed to playing the guitar feeling confident they would not produce one. Five minutes later he was playing guitar and singing songs to Morocco with their roots firmly in Andalusia.

"Wonderful," Falak screeched after the noisy applause had ended. She tried to make a comment about him juggling with fire and sword swallowing but her Arabic thoughts and Spanish words were not coordinating.

Half an hour was spent looking over the wall at Tetouan by night before reluctantly heading back inside the riad, converging on the landing of Juan's adopted bedroom and spending another ten minutes saying reluctant goodnights.

Juan closed the door behind him and dropped deadbeat onto the bed. He looked around at the grandeur of the room, at the turquoise walls and ceiling which at first glance appeared to clash with the red bedspread, yet after a short time blended in a strange, uncertain way. He looked at the open fireplace which was also painted turquoise, with a wrought iron basket jutting out at one side, containing the rough cut logs. On top of the fireplace was a huge brown dome which tapered off to a point at the top, similar to the roofs of the mosques he had seen on his way in. Three curtains hung from a pole fastened on the wall just below the ceiling. They were there for privacy but had been tied up by knotting the ends of each curtain to create three giant ball shaped knots. The bed was the biggest Juan had ever slept in. A brand new dressing gown and slippers had been carefully placed on the dark wood bedside table. A huge blue rug with intricate white designs covered most of the floor.

He laughed at the extravagance of it all. He had never been an admirer of opulence for the sake of it but this house seemed more like an extension of art, an agonisingly thought out masterpiece, meticulously put together as an important part of Morocco's mystery and history.

He finished unpacking his little rucksack, pulled on his night clothes, climbed into bed and pulled up the quilt, sniffing lung fulls of fresh winter air. He began retracing the events of his hectic day, but reached only as far as the car journey to Algejeras before sleep, deft and decisive, amiably ambushed him.

Juan woke at 9.30am after sleeping right through the night. He pulled on jeans and a shirt and danced down to the bottom of the house to see what was happening, absorbing the splendour of the house basked in natural light which instantly rekindled the joy he had said goodnight to only a few hours earlier.

Hacham and Zahra were already eating a breakfast feast of exotic fruits. They stood up and welcomed Juan and told him to help himself.

"We have to leave for Tangiers this morning Juan, I will need your help to get all your paintings together and load them into the car. The people at the gallery will hang them for us, ready for Thursday."

"I can't wait to see the gallery and also Tangiers itself. I've only been to a gallery in Malaga before this."

Hacham was beginning to realise just how little exposure and knowledge Juan had of art and its complexities. It hadn't stopped him becoming a wonderful talent though, and it somehow made the fact that he had seem even more incredible.

Juan walked towards the gallery in the house, thoughts of what was to come manifesting goose bumps. On entering the room he noticed how the pictures looked different again in the daylight, streaming sunlight pouring in through the large well positioned windows, the effect so stunning it brought a bedrock belief that the exhibition would bring him recognition, and that recognition would bring the opportunity to plant seeds of awakening to a much larger audience than he had now.

Attentively the paintings were taken down and loaded into the 4x4. Falak came running out of the house and asked if she could come too, tying up her hair and fastening her jeans as she ran.

"Have you no studying to do?" her father asked in mock stern.

"I've done all I can, I was only going to the beach with some friends anyway, I'd much rather come and see the gallery, if no one minds of course."

Juan quickly assessed his feelings, and in the few seconds it took to reach the verdict of not minding, she had already climbed in the back and was patiently waiting for the journey to commence. Zahra stayed at the house alone as Latif had already reluctantly gone to college, the same way he always went.

The journey to Tangiers took fifty minutes, taking them high up in the mountains, exposing its rugged beauty to the ever appreciative passenger.

Tangiers's seedy reputation had interested Juan ever since he began reading the works of William Burrows, Jack Kerouac, Allen Ginsberg and the other Beat writers who had all lived, visited, or just travelled through Tangiers in the 1950s. Juan relayed his literary passions to Hacham who surprised him with his knowledge of the beatniks.

"Those Beat poets and writers loved the freedom of Tangiers Juan. In that period the international city was home to both Spanish and Arab promiscuity, their sexuality was so quickly exploited in the brothels which lay in the very alleys we will soon be seeing, just behind the Grand Socco. The likes of Mr Burroughs were certainly at home here and rebellion, revolution and liberation were all cleverly cloaked in prose.

The actual name Grand Socco is another French-Spanish hybrid of course, like so many other names in Tangiers. It is claimed that Tangier's origins lie in the Grand Socco itself."

Juan stared intensely out of the window as Hacham fired information at him like an over zealous tour guide. He was buzzing with excitement by the time they dropped down from the mountains and into the centre of the city. Its chaotic traffic system was terrifying to Juan, but he soon realised it worked perfectly, even with the death wish the drivers of the cream and blue coloured Mercedes taxis carried. And every one of those taxis wore battle scars from forty odd years of unswerving loyalty to the human race.

Hacham negotiated the small streets expertly, allowing Juan only small snippets of the decaying part of Tangiers before they were prematurely confined to memory.

"Here it is Juan, here's the gallery."

The car pulled up and Juan cranked his neck to take in the full height and width of the building, its impressive design let down only by the years of grime which had taken residence on the once white walls. It was also a lot smaller than he had imagined, the word gallery had been aggrandized by Juan, tainted by the Tate and wooed by the Louvre. He looked momentarily disappointed. Hacham asked them both to stay in the car while he went to see about bringing the paintings in.

"How do you feel about all these people coming and analysing the work of your soul?"

"Terrified when you put it like that Falak."

"Well I think they are unique paintings. My dad does too; he loves it when he finds an original artist. He's like a child with a shiny coin; he won't leave you till you're completely spent."

"I really don't mind and thank you for your compliments, though I have to say painting for me is very easy. I do not find it difficult at all; therefore my talent must be questionable."

"Well I think they are far better than most of the paintings we own at home."

"I appreciate your reassuring words," he said, firing accurate arrows at the target of intimacy. "I am having a fantastic time with you and your family and I still have three days to go. I feel like a sultan wandering around your house, all that finery. You are very lucky you know, living there I mean."

"Well you could come and stay with us again, if you wanted to of course, I know my dad would love to have you back."

"And what about you?" he risked asking.

They were interrupted by the re-emergence of Hacham and his beaming smile at the window, leaving Juan guessing as to what her answer would have been.

"Some men are on their way to carry them in. Shouldn't be long, then you can come and look inside," he shouted through the glass.

Hacham opened the tail gate and began carefully taking the protective blankets from around the paintings. Juan and Falak stood and watched, happy to leave the responsibility with him. Two elderly ladies stopped and looked in at the paintings. They laughed and said something to Hacham in Arabic, wrapping and rewrapping their shawls every few seconds. Juan was intrigued by their leather like faces and he wondered what kind of life they had led here in this eclectic city of smugglers, expatriates, spies, and general villains.

They turned to Juan and one of them patted his cheek and spoke intently at him. Then they adjusted their shawls once more before heading off to live their secret lives.

Three men arrived from the gallery and negotiated the paintings inside. Their clothes were scruffy and their appearance rough, but they handled the pictures with the gentleness of new mothers. Hacham followed them through the arched doorway and into the foyer of the gallery, followed obediently by Juan and Falak. Some words were uttered to the bored looking receptionist who looked Juan up and down before a pointed finger was waved in the right direction. He looked up at the intricate designs carved into the high ceiling, art appreciation pulsating in his veins.

The gallery stretched a long way back, a much longer building than it was wide. They found the space which had been allocated to Juan and stood staring at the blankness of the walls.

"When we return your life's work will be here," Hacham noted.

"These walls will be alive."

39

CONNECTIONS

Take a look at the people you have drawn to you. Ask yourself how long you have known them for, and don't limit your mind with numeric nonsense.

They returned home in high spirits, welcomed with mint tea and warmed with a traditional meal of tagine and a fruity cous cous. The stories of the day were narrated by Hacham to Zahra.

After lunch Juan went to rest on the terrace, once more taking in all he could indulge of a city he was fast falling in love with. He was greeted shortly after by Falak carrying two bottles of beer and two glasses, spinning from one wonderful view to another.

"I thought you might like a little celebration," she said, clinking the bottles together for jubilant effect.

"What shall we celebrate? I don't want to be too presumptuous; my art career may be all over by this time next week."

"I don't think so, but we can celebrate something else if you prefer," she said, hope disguised in the casual delivery of the comment. Juan poured a beer in each glass and handed one to Falak, lifting his head and focusing on her eyes.

"What about friendship?" he asked, courageously holding her gaze. "I think we can count on that, don't you?"

"Yes I do. I can't believe it has happened so quickly, it does feel good having you around. We spoke about it last night after you had gone to bed you know; we all agreed how comfortable we felt around you."

"It's the same for me too, you feel like family already. I think we know immediately when things are meant to be."

"Does that mean we will be seeing you again?" she said, eyebrows raised and head tilted, emphasising the need for an answer.

"I hope so; we don't live so far away do we, considering we are in different continents?"

"Come on let's go and sit down," she said, linking Juan confidently and dragging out the walk to feel the closeness longer.

They sat down and began a conversation that an hour later was interrupted when Hacham and Zahra came with wine and joined them.

"I thought we might have a little celebration," Hacham said, the remark making Juan and Falak smile at the Deja vu comment.

Juan tried to suspend each moment in an attempt to elongate time. He took a mouthful of the red wine and felt the quality all the way down. He closed his eyes briefly and had a flashback of him and Alfonso sitting on the rock at the threshing ground. He remembered how his world had been tipped upside down that day, the madness, the sadness, the fear and the sheer depth of the rabbit hole he had entered. Opening his eyes again, only seconds later, he saw the immensity of the contrast in the moment he was now enjoying. He felt he had come a long way since learning the world he was living in was nothing more than a puppet theatre.

Hacham had lit the lanterns on the tables and they flickered eerily across the rooftop. It was a cold, crisp, winter night and the stars were fighting for a space to shimmer or shoot. The family had chosen their seats and nestled around Juan and Falak.

"Well, good luck Juan, we all wish you luck. There will be many other new artists at the exhibition too and a lot of interest internationally. This is the exhibition that launches many careers. I hope you are not too attached to your work, I'm certain it will all be sold. I will be making copies to print of course."

"No, if they sell that would be great. I could use the money to travel and visit more galleries, my appetite has been more than wetted by your own collection."

A cold wind was establishing itself, bullying the terrace occupants to retreat in defeat. Zahra was the first casualty, lasting only five minutes.

"I'll go down and prepare dinner," she said in Arabic, pointing at Juan in a gesture that Hacham took as "please translate to him."

The others braved the drop in temperature for a while longer, until Falak eventually asked Latif to light the two alien looking patio heaters, their obvious ugliness heightened by the stark contrast to the beauty of everything else on the terrace.

The evening meal was assaulted and after more toasts and compliments, Falak gave Juan a full tour of the riad, parts of which he still hadn't seen, including at least another three bedrooms all with entirely different colour schemes, and all finished with the meticulous eye of a gifted interior designer. Juan asked who the eye belonged to.

"My father is the guilty party. His eye for beauty is border line madness. Mum gives him a free hand in choosing everything, including all the artwork. I've no doubt one of yours will find its way into one of our rooms before you go home. Not that that's a bad thing. At least that way you won't have to leave us completely."

"Do you know something Falak; I don't think I will ever leave here fully. I need to see more of your beautiful country."

"And what about its beautiful people?" she added, her siren side fully displayed.

"Most definitely, I was hoping you could recommend a beautiful Moroccan tour guide who speaks fluent Spanish and has a good knowledge of art galleries."

"I don't know any beautiful ones, she said, negating the compliment, "I do finish university in six months though and intend travelling myself, do you think you could tolerate one so hideous to accompany such a dignified artist on his travels?" she added, escalating the fantasy.

"Yes that would perfectly acceptable. I shall return when the spring has surrendered to summer and we can gorge ourselves on history, prophecy and architecture," he said, adding fuel to the fire of frivolity.

"It's a deal then," Falak decreed, extending her hand in formal agreement and keeping a tight hold as she skipped him around more rooms, enjoying his reaction to fixtures, fittings and finery. As they flitted like children through the house they both wondered if they had really just arranged to be together for the summer.

It was 10.30 p.m. before they returned to the splendour of the main room. Hacham and Zahra had resigned themselves to the fact they had lost Juan to their perfect host of a daughter. They were happy though that they were happy.

Latif had already left to visit a friend and Falak had joined her parents while Juan walked up and down studying the paintings.

"How would you like a trip out to Chefchaouen tomorrow? It's a free day, might as well have a look around."

"I would love that, thank you. What is it?"

"A town up in the mountains, I know you will love it there Juan. It has an Andalusian feel to it but it's the light and colours which will amaze you, all whitewashed with a tint of blue and golden stone walls around its edges. I think you may want to paint it once you have seen it."

"What about you Falak, have you ever been?" he asked in an incidental tone.

"I have been once before. I'd like to see it again but I can't go tomorrow, I need to go to university and pick up some work," she told him.

Juan tried not to sound disappointed but tried too hard.

"Just us lads then?" he managed, avoiding eye contact with anyone whilst wondering how long he would be away from Falak.

The evening moved quickly and Juan was in his bed much quicker than he would have liked. The complete absence of noise and light in his room removed the option of lying there and thinking about not seeing Falak all day, prematurely ending his disappointment of a night over far too soon.

40

LIMITATION

It is possible to live a life without any limitation. This state derives not from how much one knows, but rather how much one can let go.

Jack and Florence were paying more attention to the possible outcome of Juan and Falak's meeting, tactfully dropping in on their evenings and maximising the opportunity for the five of them to be re united. Jack, Florence, Kitty, Robert and Delmore, the old team together again in a world that has long forgotten its powerful potential.

With the ability to cross dimensions by harmonising with the Earth's vibration they were able to have an aspect of themselves on Earth while another aspect was still in the realms of the afterlife. There is in fact even more possibilities on even more dimensions, a multitude of choices in a celestial adventure playground, where limitation of imagination is the only anchor.

It was after one of these visits that they decided to check on Joseph and Annie also, seduced by the memory of times when they were all together they shifted their focus towards the energy of Joseph, knowing Annie would also be found there.

The fire in the cottage was flickering; full of its own importance, burning its intention through logs and coal and making shadows dance on walls. And within these shadows two innocent intruders gate crashed the party with nothing more than a present of presence.

They saw Colleen on her Dad's knee and Joseph, well Annabelle, of course you know that, sat opposite. The shape and colour of their love travelled from one heart to the next. Conversations were read like love monitors, colour being the key factor, and the intent of the words making the vividness of colours fluctuate.

The vibration in the cottage was too seductive for Jack and Florence to stay for long and they pulled back their energy as soon as they felt all was well.

They headed to their universal home, shaped by thought, expanded by vision, and built by the courage of belief.

"It will be nice when they are all back home Florence," Jack said as they both fell into the pink softness of their chosen ethereal flower, assisting them with the recovery of cosmic travel.

"Yes it will be. Call me a sentimentalist if you like but I think we should spend longer with each other next time."

"Your loyalty to your friends should be admired, sentimentalist. There is a clear path for Delmore and Kitty to travel down. That path will also include Robert too. I hope they take it."

"We'll have to see with that one, you know Delmore with his determination to be creative. It comes first at all costs."

41

SUCCESS

Success is the determination to create, and is most alive in the creating itself. How many people clap and cheer at the result, is not of great importance.

Chefchaouen was every inch the charming village Hacham had promised, leaving Juan enchanted and with no regrets about going. The colours were striking and stimulated the already over inspired artist in Juan. So many sights captured, so much creativity niggling, bubbling restlessly in his system, waiting impatiently until an outlet to release them back into the wild is found.

They spoke about many things on the way home, Hacham pushing Juan to share more ideas and philosophies, with particular regard to his coffee and conspiracy events.

Juan was no longer surprised when most of his seemingly radical theories were accepted and agreed with by whoever he shared them with. Hacham was no exception; the depth of their conversation was a certain precursor to a deeper friendship. Time condensed itself on that homeward trip, pinching a conversation here, an observation there, cutting short the experience of travel and companionship, leaving them both asking where it had gone. And as they walked into the courtyard laughing like schoolboys; it was only the sight of Falak and Zahra enjoying an afternoon swim that popped their bubble of brotherhood.

"Hey come and join us," Falak shouted, elated at their return.

"Ok let me get changed, I won't be a minute. Are you coming Hacham?"

"Yes why not, I'll see you back here in a moment. Are you alright for swim wear?"

"Yeah got shorts in the house," Juan shouted, already heading there.

The pool was heated to the perfect temperature, naturally, and Juan dived straight in, losing his mountain dust in one underwater length, resurfacing a refreshed man. He swam over to Falak and Zahra and took questions on the topic of his trip to Chefchaouen.

Hacham arrived after five minutes with a bottle of red wine in one hand and fluffy white towels under his other arm. He walked over to the alcove and brought four glasses across to the side of the pool.

"We will swim first and relax after," he said, pouring the wine in preparation.

Juan was becoming acclimatised to the flamboyant lifestyle and found himself thinking more and more about when he might return here. The trip in summer he'd vaguely arranged with Falak had neither been confirmed or spoke about since. He knew he would have to ask again and risk the chance of finding out that she was actually acting out a scene from an imaginary love story, and not serious about the arrangement in the real world. (Real world being open to interpretation of course.) But for now Juan was nestled in the beauty of the moment, a moment which had far more in common with fiction than fact. He would deal with the facts of the fiction later.

After a few lengths and tread watered conversation the four of them retired to the side of the pool, staying there for around an hour, shoulders below the surface of the water for necessary warmth.

Zahra and Hacham were first out, trading pleasure for practicality and confirming their intention to get ready for the evening meal. Falak had no such desire and chose to stay until circumstance forced her otherwise, trying to drown Juan by swinging on his shoulders, using the pretence of play to justify a physical closeness that would otherwise not be permitted. And in the midst of those wrestled cuddles and non-accidental brushes, a continuity plan was telepathically sent from internal outbox's to internal inbox's.

Now and again life turns in a dazzling performance with no effort needed and this was one of those weeks for Juan; a memory in the making for when he can no longer experience the reality, through old age or incapacity or whatever other experience or agreement awaits him. And when that time arrives, these breathtaking memories will be more than sufficient.

Hacham chose a local restaurant for their evening meal, a time honoured and staunchly traditional eatery, ten minutes walk from the house. The atmosphere between the family was one of hi jinx, the following day's exhibition being one of the reasons, the collapsing of ego boundaries and the genuine empathy between them being the other. The friendships built that evening on the back drop of culture and cuisine, were formed, enhanced, labelled eternal, and cemented with a mix, two parts respect to one part honour.

After the meal they walked for sixteen minutes in the pitch black to their home, five full bellies graciously taking the blame for the extra six minutes. The streets were busy with other diners, families out for walks and the global challenge of youths looking for places to perform pubescent posturing.

Back inside the house Zahra was making the mint tea which Juan was finally getting used to and almost enjoying, well, almost. He and Latif were deep in conversation regarding styles, periods, art and artists. This was the first time they had engaged at a level deeper than a scratched surface. Latif's confidence in speaking Spanish was growing the more he understood and the more he made himself understood.

Hacham and Falak had driven into Tetouan to collect the prints of Juan's paintings. A friend and fellow art enthusiast had been enrolled to make the copies, telling Hacham they would cause a storm at the exhibition as he handed them over, wrapped in cellophane and cotton sheets.

When dad and daughter returned they found Juan playing guitar and singing by the pool, Zahra and Latif listening with the intensity of a cat stalking a bird. He cut short the song and went over to Hacham and Falak, partly for the prints, mostly for Falak. Hacham put them down on the table and removed the sheets, revealing the much anticipated results. Once again they shocked Juan, different light, different material, random order, all removing his familiarity and giving him the opportunity of a first time viewer.

"Listen Juan," he said, saddened by the cold necessity of organisation. "We need to leave around eight in the morning; I'd like to be there well before it opens at ten, get the feel for the place you know, the atmosphere, it builds throughout the day, you're going to love it Juan. But for now I will say goodnight to you my friend and look forward to tomorrow. Sleep well now."

"Thank you for all you have done, this has been the best week of my life," Juan replied, shaking hands with one and waving a thank you to Zahra with the other.

Hacham caught up with her and they left the pool area hand in hand, almost skipping with delight. The remaining three sat for a while before fatigue made legs twitch and eyes burn.

Lying on his bed, surveying the splendour of his bedroom, he thought about his great fortune to be here, living in this freedom and abundance. He imagined how life would be for him if tomorrow all the success that Hacham had convinced him would come, did in fact materialise, how he could focus on his paintings as his source of income and still have time to concentrate on his campaign to spread information throughout the world, knowing that information was the only difference between suppression and enlightenment, even if that information was just that we are already all knowing.

He thought also how he would have the time and resources to finally achieve the optimum diet that would nourish his whole system and bring life to his body instead of premature death, and even how he might take up the wonderful art of Aikido, just like his friend in the mountains once practiced. He visualised his life being lived in accordance to all universal laws and felt he was beginning to know many things, a different feeling than his previous thought based knowing though; he felt it somewhere near the heart. He eventually fell asleep in contemplation of such things.

42

MANIFESTATION

Every thought sets off a multitude of possibilities, even new life. They are the beginning of everything you manifest. Think about what you think about.

Alarms rang between 6 and 7a.m. Juan ironically was the last one up, suffering his worst night sleep so far. Absolute silence and jet black darkness had proved no match for excitement and apprehension. Fruit and mint tea were available in the dining room, functioning as a grab and go service. The morning bore witness to quick showers, dressing in motion, and snippets of conversations carrying polite instruction.

By 8.30am Juan was sitting comfortably in the front of the Mercedes, the same car that had brought him from Algarrobo only a few days ago. He re acquainted himself with the smell, sound, and feel of that exquisite piece of German craftsmanship, struggling to convince himself that he had only been in Morocco for a handful of hours. He had left Spain behind with his physical, mental, and spiritual totality, barely thinking about his home since leaving.

Ironically none of the conversation on the way to Tangiers was about the exhibition, as though all the words had been used up in their pre match talk and the only thing that was left to do was play the game out.

Juan was surprisingly calm for a day that would change his world. He wore dark jeans, sandals, and the only shirt he had brought which Zahra had wrestled off him earlier and sentenced to a spell on the ironing board. His jet black hair was pinned back by the sunglasses on his head. Juan certainly looked on the outside every inch of the interesting character he was on the inside.

They sped through the green countryside, passing old farms, old people, goats, and the odd camel.

Tangiers crept up slowly, teasing with its peripheries one moment, and then bursting into full bloom with its exploding chaotic centre the next.

The streets were busy with early commuters, nipping in and out of the cafes, which had facilitated the same needs of mankind decade after decade. Tea sipped, cigarettes smoked, food nibbled, newspapers glanced over, and small talk exchanged as Tangier began a brand new morning.

Inside the art gallery a gentle buzz was already present, a mixture of formal suits and ties mingled with the more bohemian attire of the artists, who were thinking only in terms of credibility, the suits and ties of course, thinking only in currency, one room, two worlds, always the case.

Hacham was greeted by almost everyone in the gallery. A pride filled Juan quickly realised just how revered he was in the world of art. He hadn't disclosed the depth of his influence to him, preferring to just let things unfold and be revealed in their own time.

The five of them made their way to Juan's allocated section, his excitement growing with each step, quickening the pace; arriving at the very same place they had been standing a few days before with eyes of anticipation, gazing longingly at a blank wall.

"Wow," Juan said, surveying the final result of thought made manifest. The full force of what was occurring caught him with guard lowered, no warning jabs, straight knock out. He had no idea what it felt like to be in a gallery with his own works on display, he was lost in new territory with no reference point. Falak realised he was floundering and slipped a reassuring hand into his. It was enough to lift him from the canvas and recover enough to fight on. He took a deep breath, spun around and guided her to all the other displays, spending only seconds at each one, laser eyes making little left-right sweeps, assessing all of his competition in less than two minutes. They arrived back at Juan's display to find no one else had moved.

"Well, what do you think? Now do you believe you are worthy of a place in here?"

"Yes I think so. They are all great in different ways aren't they? I'll look some more later, just wanted to see, you know how it is?"

"Of course I know how it is, let's go and get a drink and meet some of the other artists, I'll translate if you need me," she said, enjoying the "need me" line.

They spent the next hour doing that, meeting the artists, introductions via Hacham, and then taking them over to his own work, almost apologetically showing them his offerings. And every time he encountered the same inspired response. It shocked him when he finally came out of those engrossed introductions and looked up, what with the gallery filling up so quickly and all.

Individuals and groups of people were forming their secret opinions of the works on display. Juan tried his hand at being a body language expert, desperate to read any tell tale signs of approval in pulled faces, animated gestures, and pensive stances.

Hacham's mobile phone rang and he temporarily disappeared, Zahra and Latif dutifully following. Falak stuck to Juan's side, partly in protection and partly in devotion. She wanted to be there throughout the whole day, watching the seed of an unknown artist flower in public.

"We don't have to stand here all day do we?" Juan asked, not wishing to be tied to his paintings by protocol.

"No, some of the artists are not even coming today. Let's stay for a while longer though, I love seeing peoples reaction when they see your work, I find it fascinating."

Falak quizzed him some more, Juan tried to answer every question on the inspirations and applications of each of his paintings, with Falak in the mock role of interviewer. He asked her a question of his own.

"Where did your Father go?"

She told him it was probably a business call and was adding to the assumption when her own phone began to ring. She moved away from Juan to take the quick call, then her soft hand found the small of his back and he was ushered to another of his paintings to ask yet another probing question. Juan did his best to show her how he used texture to obtain the feeling of depth, satisfactorily answering the question, unaware of the moment in waiting.

The voice came from somewhere behind his left shoulder.

"Not bad for an amateur."

Juan spun around to find a familiar face, yet a face that took a few seconds to register with his brain. The hair was long, grey, and tied up. He had a matching grey beard which denied Juan the instant recognition, but then . . .

"Alfonso," he shouted, much louder than he had wished.

"Yes, it is I indeed. The mountain lunatic is here in Tangier. You didn't think I would miss an event like this did you?"

"I didn't think you were this interested in art," he said, recovering well enough from the outlandish moment to deliver an average observation.

"I'm not really, but I am interested in you, your paintings are fantastic but your greetings are lousy," and he threw his arms out for Juan to fall into. They hugged, squeezed, and patted backs before stepping out, catching each other's elbows and looking each other up and down.

"How did you know about it? How did you know I was here? Where are you staying?"

"All will be revealed in time. My good friend Hacham and his beautiful family are more secretive than you may have given them credit for," he informed, eyes twinkling with mischief.

Hacham, Zahra and Latif had been watching the event from the edge of the gallery, their careful planning culminating in the re union now unfolding.

"How did you meet them?" Juan said, forgetting about their trip to Aljibe.

"We have kept in touch since their visit in the summer. I knew Hacham was a man of his word. It was obvious to me he would assist you on your life journey."

"I can't believe they called in your restaurant that day, of all the places in those mountains," Juan said.

"No coincidence of course. And I hope you haven't forgotten to thank the invisible forces who have seen you through to this point?"

Juan was transported back to Las Alpujarras and his experience there, just listening to that voice, its powerful intention and the way it seemed to hit on many more levels than the audible one, rolling back the years. Then he looked at that face, steeped in character, hardly changed in six years, and just for a moment he actually thought he got a scent of that mountain air. He shook his head in sheer disbelief, unable to resist giving Alfonso another hug.

"Come on young man, let's go and get some drinks and leave your paintings to sell themselves," he said, dancing a quick jig which ended with him linking Juan and spinning him in the direction of the door.

Noisy conversations bounced between tenement walls as the six of them headed off to the Gran café de Paris, just behind the Grand Socco. Falak utilised the merriment and slipped her hand into Juan's almost unnoticed, almost except for an ultra observant wizard who merely gave Juan a smirk and a wink.

"You really must thank your guides Juan, I think they have been very busy," he said teasingly.

Alfonso and Hacham had kept in contact by telephone since their meeting, Hacham keeping him informed almost daily during the last two weeks of Juan's whereabouts, arrangements for the exhibition, even describing his appearance and dress style to an ever attentive Alfonso.

Alfonso had had no hesitation accepting the invite to come to the exhibition and to stay over at their house, making his way by coach and boat, arriving in Tangiers by taxi and booking into a small hotel nearby. He had accepted Hacham's kind offer to take him back to Spain with Juan the morning after too.

"Mint teas all round is it?" Alfonso laughed. "I bet you would wrestle a lion for an espresso eh Juan?"

Juan noticed Alfonso had seemed to have lost his posture since he last saw him, slouching at the table was something he was sure he never did back then and he couldn't resist commenting on it.

"Posture Alfonso," he grinned. "How can you connect with the energies of the universe in this crumpled position?" he added, adding another two inches to his own to safe guard his observation.

"I see you have taken my advice on board Juan. I do hope you haven't become a new age snob though."

"How do you mean Alfonso?" Juan replied, mildly perplexed.

"You know, new age often being the last bouncer at the door to freedom, with it's thirty affirmations, six times daily to guarantee cosmic results, spinning clockwise twenty one times to bring you closer to God, meditating with a pyramid on your head, you know what I'm talking about, goody two shoes in the lotus position."

"But you always said…."

"Never mind all of that. Do you think just because you weigh twenty seven stone you cannot access infinite consciousness or be a master of unconditional love? Can a paralysed person not align with God because his posture is wrong? Do you need to lay out your crystals in the shape of a merkaba before you can feel a part of infinity?"

"Why did you teach such things to me then?" Juan said, already regretting his casual remark.

"They were meant only as guides, points of focus until you felt it naturally. Of course I am not saying it is not good to have alignment and correct posture, of course it is, staying centred is very beneficial, but it does not give you exclusivity, the infinite everything does not give out bonus points to those with the most crystals and singing bowls. Trinkets Juan, that's all they are, workings of the mind, nothing more. Be careful, that's all I'm saying. Having to shave your head and wear the correct purple tunic is just mind work, illusion in other words. The new age movement often highlights and criticises the dogma of religion and its rule books while creating its own set of structured nonsense. Some of it is fine, don't misunderstand me, but a lot of it is a dangerous diversion. We are already infinite energy, we have nothing to align to in that sense, we are already it. And understanding that you are all that is, has ever been and will ever be, and that you're not your mind, body, ego, name, or the pins and needles in your legs from too much sitting in the lotus position, will give you true understanding. Here come the drinks."

They sat down and told the stories of how they had successfully managed to coordinate the event. Juan wanted to know everything about the restaurant in the mountains and just what Alfonso had been doing with the six years that were sandwiched by their two meetings.

"Nothing has changed there much Juan," he told him. "You may however have noticed that I have been transforming my appearance into that of a Hollywood film star," he said, which set him off on one of his outbursts of seemingly inappropriate laughter, made more noticeable by the fact they were in a small restaurant packed with people, as opposed to an isolated old threshing ground.

There was a truth however in his statement; he did look somewhat of a film star, the greying hair and white beard, stark in contrast to his dark coloured suit and highlighted by a cleverly chosen white polo neck, were definite signs of a man who knew how to impress.

What Alfonso lacked in height he made up for in presence, filling any room he entered with the powerful aura he carried, captivating all who set eyes upon him.

They sipped tea and enthusiastically tried the variety of little cakes that teased and tantalised them from their display trolley, oblivious of time, until Hacham, the unelected group leader, noticed that an hour had already sneaked through their time zone, one illusion outwitting another.

They paid up and headed back to a packed, vociferous gallery. Hacham checked with the organiser and then delivered the news to Juan that most of his paintings were already sold. After the week he had experienced, the news, however life changing, did not impact on him as it may have done in less prolific times. In fact, it didn't even match that surprise reunion with Alfonso, or drinking red wine with Falak on the rooftop overlooking Tetouan.

"Well Juan, I guess the universe is yours," Alfonso said, displaying his irresistible grin, teeth flashed, dimples displayed.

Juan went on to speak to the film crews and magazine and newspaper journalists who were sniffing around for exclusive titbits. Flashlights flashed, mobiles rang, and Juan tentatively entered the world of a rock star.

Latif helped once more to translate as they tried to extract everything from his inspirations to his philosophies. He disappointed on the first account but excelled on the second, and Juan Santiago (my great friend Delmore) would soon begin to infiltrate the art world, having found a medium to convey his thoughts and feelings, a way of expressing the beauty he saw in what most people found unremarkable. He had always looked for the beauty in things and through his pursuit and continual appreciation of it; he was now actually living in it.

A few more questions answered and contacts established brought the first day of the exhibition to a close. It had been a clockwork success engineered by an invisible hand, and the invisible hand in the main belonged to Soran. He had been brought in to assist in Juan's wish to work with his creativity, the perfect guide for that particular field, assisting him whole heartedly to his highest spiritual evolution. All Juan had done was declare his intent, ask for guidance, and lock on like a laser beam to his target.

The six of them squashed into the car, Juan looking through the back window and wringing out the last drops of euphoria as the gallery disappeared round corners and behind buildings.

He remembered how as a child he did the same thing on leaving the village of Methina Fondales. Now the cause of that sadness was sat in the front of the car he was now travelling in, and the car was off to a palace in Morocco where they would be spending a night never to be forgotten.

Juan felt as though this night would be the highlight of the whole trip, a culmination of his life so far, a closure of all things previous as well as a new beginning. He didn't however; know the full extent to which his life would be changing.

The ride home was one of great excitement and celebration, only marred by the fleeting and niggling thought that constantly gate crashed his joy, reminding the owner of it that tomorrow the dream would all be over.

Back at home Alfonso grinned through his guided tour of the house, hands behind his back, erect in posture and bouncing his way from room to room.

Hacham equally enjoyed the tour and delighted in the responses his new friend offered. Juan stayed by his side, making up in some small way for the six years he had been denied contact.

"What a wonderful manifestation of your thoughts," he finally said, surveying the whole riad from the courtyard. "You are very worthy of this magnificent home too," he added.

"Everyone else says we are lucky, you certainly think about your words Alfonso."

"I believe thought forms, words, feelings, intentions and belief patterns are so critical in the world we have built around us. I see no purpose in building an ugly one. It's obvious you don't either," Alfonso said.

"Do you live in similar affluence Alfonso?"

"Yes I am surrounded by beauty also, albeit the beauty of nature. I do not have much to take care of however, just a couple of rooms above the restaurant. But yes, I live in great beauty all the same. As complex as I may appear with my riddles and such, I am actually a very simple man, you could write down my philosophy of life on a postage stamp."

"What set you off on the path of the spirit initially?" Hacham asked, with a genuine intrigue.

"I was born with a curious mind Hacham, I came in with it. The search for truth was a burning ember I held tightly in my hand. Very much like our Juan here. That is why I have great interest in your progression Juan," he said, squeezing his knee to let him know the subject had shifted to him.

"I knew you were coming up to the mountains before you got there. I haven't mentioned it before but I have acquired the little gift of clairvoyance, I know we have been together before Juan. When I first met you I felt it was important to help you and set you off on the path you are now on, you too Hacham. I am not too certain of the particulars but we are all in this adventure together, a meeting of old souls with a clear mission if you like."

"Well you're never short of surprises are you?" Hacham laughed.

Juan could only offer a smile and a shake of his head."

Zahra killed the Meta physical moment by calling the three of them in for their evening meal, prepared meticulously by herself and Falak, Latif assisting them in his own way.

The meal was followed by organic wine, bought specially by Zahra who had remembered Alfonso's little speech in the mountain restaurant. Alfonso turned toastmaster once more.

"May I thank you all for the wonderful day and evening we have shared. Juan, you have had a successful day today, I do not have to tell you not to let it change you. It is merely an experience and I know you have a fine head on your shoulders. Use your good fortune to serve your fellow man. Put some goodness into the planet and make a difference. This will not be the first time we will be toasting together. Another event is coming soon, but I must not let a glass of wine loosen my tongue too much," he said, pinching his tongue for double effect.

"I know you will join me Juan in thanking our hosts for making this day so memorable. You must have had a wonderful few days here."

He looked to Juan for agreement. It came in the nod of a head and a smile aimed at each member of the family.

"So shall we toast the fact that somehow, through a universe we can't get to the end of we find ourselves here in this room together for this microcosm of time?"

He lifted his glass, stuck his chest out, feet pushed firmly together and announced. "To our never ending journey."

The phrase was para phrased in Arabic and clinking glasses cemented the sentiment.

They finished off the night on the rooftop, Alfonso staring up at the sky looking for a clue to his existence, Hacham pondering the line between genius maverick and crazy eccentric. Zahra and Latif were cuddled on the huge sofa making Juan momentarily think of home and his family. He and Falak were sitting together on the sofa too, wondering where their compasses were pointing.

It was Hacham and Zahra who declared their fatigue first, heading downstairs towards the lure of their luxurious bed. Latif soon joined them, the intensity of a day like that would naturally take its prisoners. Hugs and handshakes were generously given and received. Alfonso, Juan and Falak were left to fly the flag of frivolity for as long as they could manage, a mere five minutes registered for Alfonso.

"I'm afraid my soul is ready to return to the celestial plane for rest and a recharge," he casually said, joining his hands at the chest and bowing firstly to his friends, then out across the terrace to Morocco, Mercury, and maybe even further. "I will leave you two to act out the final scene of your illusory drama. It's been a wonderful day and we must be thankful for the beauty we have kindly been shown. Goodnight my dear friends."

"Goodnight Alfonso," they said together.

Falak followed him down and escorted him to his room.

"Remember the path has been cleared," he said, firing a thought provoking shot of departure.

When she arrived back on the rooftop with nightcap coffee, she found Juan looking over at the view once more, digesting all he could of the night lights of Tetouan, almost breathing in the orange glow with concentration.

"I've brought us a drink up Juan, maybe our last one together."

"Last one for now of course, don't forget you offered your service as a tour guide in the summer. I hope you were serious, I've been planning my route all week."

This was the best Juan could come up with spontaneously. He felt the statement carried the intention clearly enough, yet retained enough humour to imply he was fooling around if she did refute the suggestion, and the frail craft of the ego would not be sunk. Her response did far more than just keep boats afloat.

"I really don't want to wait until summer; I can't imagine our home without you in it now."

Juan had been shown a safety net and wasted no time in taking that leap.

"Maybe Alfonso was implying something when he spoke about the final part of our drama."

"Alfonso was more than implying, he believes it's our destiny."

Juan took the drinks from her and walked to the table to set them down. He then returned to where she was standing and extended both hands with a marginal degree of confidence. They were instantly met by Falak's, which he used as two levers to manoeuvre her to him before finishing off with an over anticipated and immensely intense hug. The hug was replaced by a first kiss, timeless and with no concern of being overlong, a complete abandonment of restriction and restraint, a merging of urges and desires. Once the permission had been granted, no further invitation was issued or required and they got to know as much about each other as is possible in the minutes they were presented with. The freedom to explore coupled with the urgency to fit five days worth of suppressed feelings in, saw the understandable demise of the spoken word. The blanket wrapped around them lost the battle at three am to a dispassionate temperature drop. They headed back into the warmth of the house which seemed surprisingly different to Juan, due to his change of circumstances on the roof. He was used to seeing its décor through the eyes of a man living his life alone; things looked very different however through the eyes of a shared soul. He mused how in the space of a minute he had made the leap from vulnerable to wonderful.

"I think we better get some sleep," Falak said, with the one rational brain cell left, and that goodnight kiss robbed them of a further thirty minutes.

43

SYNCHRONICITY

The moment you put your attention and focus to something, a thousand future events are called into action. You will surely meet them down the time line and call them coincidence.

So synchronicity, design, cause and effect and destiny had played their parts impeccably, while chance, coincidence and luck however, although often mentioned, were never really in the equation.

Juan and Falak were on a new journey now, Alfonso had honoured his promise and Joseph and Annie were successfully achieving their personal goals in the form of Annabelle and Colleen, as close as both of them had hoped for pre incarnation.

Jack and Florence, content with being two cosmic drifters were enjoying coming and going, merging with other light beings, learning new depths of consciousness and travelling on a vehicle called intent. It was wonderful to be free of the heavy mind and body density, at least for a while anyway. They were happy to be coaching from the cosmic sidelines, helping out whenever they were called on.

From this acute state of awareness they could very clearly see that planet Earth had indeed been hijacked from the time when its population had lived in accordance with universal laws. Great technological advancements over the last few centuries had certainly advanced the physical development immeasurably, but a turning away from nature and the mother Earth herself, and, to be fair, an outside attack of the human perception had left the planet spiritually retarded.

Now there is real fear in the heart of mankind, a fear of impending change, a realisation that this era of self serving materialism and reptilian like control is coming to an end and the beginning of a more spiritually balanced age is on its way. The fear is present as the old era will not be leaving without a fight, and climatic disasters, war, famine, and the last throws of human negativity are testing and threatening the very existence of mankind. The evil hand that holds the puppet strings in the theatre of nightmares called existence, shown daily in all its different guises, has seemingly claimed a victory.

The victory however, when viewed through the narrow lenses of a third dimensional illusion and five sense limitation was nothing more than a premature assumption. The gift of vision now experienced by Jack and Florence allowed them to see that the seeds of desire and a new way of thinking had been planted.

The success of the coming revolution would be its ability to create a new vision for the planet by enough people and hold on steadfast as its awareness expanded and spiralled outwards to reach a critical mass or tipping point. A collection of light carriers were switching on throughout the Earth, reminding everyone they encountered that there is another way of living their Earth life.

This was another reason Jack and Florence were working so closely with Juan, opening doors and removing the obstacles that would otherwise slow down the progress. Time was running out in one sense and the willing carriers of the torch of light needed to fly.

Juan had understood this necessary plan, informing people of the tyranny and quickly moving them on to a place of renewed hope, encouraging them to hold on to the vision of how they wanted the world to be rather than dwelling on how it was. He knew this was powerful enough to flip the evolution of the planet. He didn't know how or why it would work, but it resonated as a truth in his heart.

I've just checked with my cosmic editor and he will allow me to say that the figure of around fifteen percent could be sufficient to create a new paradigm; you know the five hundred monkey thing don't you? So it may be that you are already very close.

Juan tried to convey these ideas in his paintings too, sometimes overtly, other times subliminally, leaving the viewer to not necessarily decode, but to realise that there was another path that was available for them or at least another way of viewing the world they lived in. It wasn't important to Juan if the subliminal was correctly interpreted, but more that a general feeling of hope was conveyed.

He had come to the same conclusion with the crop circles he had developed such a passion for, that maybe it is important to decode them or maybe not, but the message that should be embraced is the fact that you have external help to balance the Earth. You are a planet of free will, but you are not completely alone in this battle.

44

DECISIONS

Make them with your instinct and move on quickly. Don't let your head interfere.

The sun came up strong, a ball of gold in an already aqua blue sky, prematurely stirring the occupants of the house and an unwelcome intrusion to an unwanted morning.

It was going to be a difficult day with the sadness of farewells, the cloud of departure already overshadowing any attempt to inject joviality into breakfast. It had been a monumental week in Juan's life and no amount of fresh fruit and architectural elegance could make the idea of leaving it all behind seem like a good thing to do.

It was Alfonso who reminded Juan that opportunities should always be seized and love should never wait, pulling Juan close to him as he imparted more wisdom, adopting his more monotone pitch, the one he always chose for more serious moments.

"Any decision you make in the next thirty minutes will have far reaching consequences. With five minutes of honest dialogue you and Falak can create any outcome you desire, starting this very day. You appear to be accepting the wrong assumption that separating is your only option. If you don't want suffering to be part of your movie then write a different scene. Remember Juan, you are the writer, the director and the actor, you own the script. No copyright issues. There is absolutely no reason you should let anyone else write your movie."

The result of this conversation was the reason Falak was sat in the car with them two hours later. Conversations between Juan, Alfonso, and the family had culminated in them going to stay the following week at his house in Spain. A condensed phone call to his mum and dad was the only preparation they were offered for accepting the stranger he already loved into their home.

Juan left Morocco that morning the only way he could have envisaged, by taking a chunk of it home with him.

Hacham, the one with the with whirling emotions, had to say goodbye to them briefly in Algarrobo before driving on to Las Alpujarras once more, safely delivering Alfonso to his beloved mountains. In just a few days he had discovered an artist, found a friend and welcomed a future son in law into his life. The smile he wore had elements of irony and disbelief, but mostly was made up of inexplicable joy.

A quick turn around saw him back at Juan's home in under three hours, staying overnight and heading back home the day after, taking full advantage of the opportunity to get to know Juan's family and also his own to be, a surreal experience for the under prepared recipients of unstoppable love.

Juan spent the next year travelling between Tetouan and his own home. He continued with his "Coffee and Conspiracy" meetings but broke the numbers down into smaller groups, giving more responsibility to his friends and others to set up their own meetings in different venues, allowing for the law of leverage to have its multiplying effect. His idea that it would only take a certain amount of people and not the whole planet to wake up and detach from the "New World Order" was making more sense to more people.

He did all his painting in the Moroccan house where Hacham had created an inspiring room to work in with his favourite view across Tetouan. Juan counted his blessings almost hourly, not only for the creative splendour of his surroundings but equally for acquiring a father in law with such tailor made attributes. (I know from my own experience this is not always the case!)

His credibility and fame continued to grow and as he travelled between Spain and Morocco he naturally dropped his "wake up" seeds on all he connected with, just as he had planned to.

Falak and Juan were married in Tangiers within a year, the families coming together and spending three days in a hotel in the centre of the city. Falak and Juan spent a great deal of their time in the Kasbah in the old part of Tangier, absorbing the synergistic blend of spices, prayer calls, hashish, history, and enjoying the continuing emotional battle between fear and excitement.

Alfonso made the trip too. He stayed with them the week before the wedding, being treated to day trips out and personalised tours of the highlights of the region, their friendship growing deeper, and Alfonso, the one time semi recluse, thoroughly enjoying his renewed enthusiasm for travel.

After the three days in Tangiers, Falak and Juan went on to Rabat and the most Moroccan of all the cities, Fez. The honeymoon lasted three weeks, the period of goodwill much longer. Juan then returned home to Algarrobo, begrudgingly leaving Falak with her family for a whole week. He spent the time catching up with his own family and friends and focusing on his work at the café.

His life had changed almost beyond recognition but he still had fire in his belly for peaceful rebellion, still marching fearlessly into the eye of the storm.

Travel was to be the essence of their lives for a considerable time, the hostility of passport control losing its power as they trudged between the two countries, learning each others languages, devouring history and destroying division with nothing more than a heart full of love.

45

LAUGHTER

Humour can be found in most situations and laughter is free therapy for the soul. So sack your psychiatrist and watch a good comedy film instead. Better still, laugh at your psychiatrist, they've always seemed like a funny bunch to me.

Later that year, that year with a day, a month, and a set of numbers attached, that same year that tricked them into believing time is a fixed, immovable, sequence of events, that very year that will hear nothing of the claim that future and past can be changed by consciousness, yes, that year, during a stay at Juan's house, Juan and Falak decided to pay Alfonso a surprise visit in the mountains, a personal hankering of Juan's to indulge in the nostalgia of that life changing holiday he innocently embarked upon had recently started to hound him.

Mild curiosity had developed into full blown excitement as the time for their departure neared and he had allowed himself the previously denied indulgence of memory recall.

He had always refused the post mortem of that experience in the mountains; especially when he wasn't sure if he would ever return. Now he was actually enjoying delving into those deep seated emotions, teasing them to the surface with the seductive bait of reconnection.

Juan had never been inside Alfonso's living quarters. He only knew it was above the restaurant in a couple of rooms the owner had allowed him to use to make the running of the restaurant more practicable.

It was bright and sunny when they pulled up in Falak's car. Aljibe was exactly as he had remembered, the familiarity stirring strong feelings in Juan, unnerving one moment and thrilling the next. They entered the restaurant wearing two huge grins in anticipation of the surprise on Alfonso's face. The room was in semi darkness and eerily quiet. Juan took the lead role and shouted Alfonso as he walked round the back of the bar, finding a staircase which he nervously climbed and signalling for Falak to follow.

He was calling his name every third or forth step now, the tone changing from inquisitive to imperative. They saw a half open door across the landing and using only facial gestures agreed to proceed.

The light from the window revealed the outline of a body under the covers on a thin mattress in the corner of the room. Juan called his name once more, breaking the silence momentarily, as two sets of eyes met briefly to agree on the seriousness of the moment. Suddenly the excitement was gone and in its place was an unwelcome fear, which left them feeling a little silly about their trivial trick.

Juan breathed deeply and held that breath while he hesitantly walked to the bed and gently shook the shape beneath the covers. No response. He shook harder, gently calling his name.

Falak, still standing in the doorway shook her head forlornly at Juan, as he fumbled for the edge of the blanket, taking another deep breath to help him through the next few dreadful moments.

"Can I be of some assistance to you?" the voice boomed from the landing, only a metre away from where Falak stood.

Juan dropped the blanket and spun around to see Falak with two hands covering a gaping mouth, and Alfonso laughing in his unmistakable way behind her.

"Surprise," he then yelled, setting him off on another bout of hysteria, lasting long enough for the two of them to breathe fully once more.

"What are you doing, you nearly killed us?" Juan said, with a mixed tone of anger and relief.

"I could have," he replied, "you are in my room."

"We came to surprise you but you weren't in the bar. We thought you were..."

"I know what you thought, and of course that adds to the comedy. Now then, let me get you some water. It is wonderful as always to see you both by the way. Please wait here and make yourself comfortable. Don't sit on my guest though; I think he's still asleep."

Juan couldn't resist pulling back the covers once Alfonso had gone downstairs. He quickly walked over to the bed and whipped them back to reveal nothing more than a thick quilt bunched up with a pillow at the top, obviously shaped to resemble a human. For what reason they didn't even try to guess.

Alfonso returned with two glasses of water which he put down on a one metre square wooden board, held up by a pile of books at either end. Juan looked at the makeshift coffee table and smiled to himself, forgetting that nothing escaped the attention of Alfonso's trained eyes.

"My simplicity should not surprise you Juan. I need nothing that will not serve me functionally."

They both looked around the room with minimum movement of their heads. There was the bed in the corner, some straw mats scattered around the floor covering some very old rustic tiles, an antique cabinet with an old picture of sensei Morihei Ueshiba dressed in a black Hakama and pointing a sword outwards from his chest, to the obvious destiny of infinity.

A single chair sat in one corner, tucked under a small desk with papers strewn all over it, and probably his only modern possession, a half decent hi-fi system. Underneath the window was a pile of around thirty books. Juan scanned them to see if he could make out the titles of any. He saw Japanese gardens, tea making ceremonies, a book on house maintenance; teach yourself French, and a guide book about food and water storage. His curiosity would bring him back to the rest of the books later, believing he would learn more about what kind of a man Alfonso was by a sneaky glance at the books he owned.

"Where is your television?" Juan asked, smirking in anticipation of Alfonso's answer.

"I don't own one, I haven't watched one for over twenty years. It's the work of the devil for certain. Mass mind control would be so much more difficult without the little screen in every living room of the entire planet. Think about that for a moment. Firstly they are able to dumb down your intelligence with programmes that wouldn't stimulate a six year old child. For example you can be subjected to a chat show where some idolised film star is interviewed and given a standing ovation at the end just because he strung some sentences together. Or maybe a nice film to seduce your thoughts a little more. Then we have music to disturb and distort your chemical balance, deliberately tuned to a pitch that is out of resonance with human oscillation, absolutely never 528 hertz my good people."

Alfonso stepped backwards and kicked an imaginary football, throwing his hands up as the shot from his fancy footwork hit the back of a fantasy net.

"How about watching a nice game of football to stimulate your hostility towards your fellow man? Of course you could always go to the stadium to watch the game, well that's if you're affluent of course. It's a bit out of reach for the average working family but I guess it has to be like that. They wouldn't be able to pay those hard working players thousands of pounds per week if they didn't charge so much to enter the stadium. Think of this for a moment. It may cost a family a quarter of their weekly income to watch the men kick a ball on some grass and earn themselves over three thousand times their weekly income in ninety minutes. And we stand for this.

Don't misunderstand me here, football is a beautiful game, beautiful, but it's like everything else on the planet, it's been hijacked by criminals.

What about a daily dose of your favourite soap opera, a wonderful guide of how to run your family?

Then there is the bad news at one, the bad news at six, the bad news at ten, in fact every minute of the day there is a news channel to serve your daily dose of depression and feed you a diet of lies and propaganda. What a clever invention the television was, a most useful tool to serve the ruling elite. Switch on and see the masses of people waving flags at the president responsible for a million deaths. WAKE UP, WAKE UP, WAKE UP!" he yelled at a half open window, to a half awake world.

236

Alfonso walked over and patted his pile of books.

"You must be ruthless with your discretion about what you feed your mind on. I do not live in the same world as most people. Every day I see the results of my positive outlook on life and every day I show gratitude for the things I do have, and if I don't like what I have, I'm thankful for the opportunity to transform it and transcend it. This is the secret to healing the planet. Transcend my friend," he said, lifting his arms up to the sky and smiling at another goal scored.

"There is much work taking place as you know, we are not alone in our effort to transcend our current situation and create a new paradigm. The difficulty of course, is in the measuring. We have no way of knowing where we are up to, but still, we have a plan. The oppressors have their plan and we have ours. And the secret is our plan does not oppose their plan physically, it merely TRANSCENDS IT," he said in massively exaggerated tones.

"It is no use focusing all your energy opposing this plan of negativity. It is imperative that we get over it and create a new thing. Out with the old and in with the new. You will see great disruption to your planet in the months and years ahead. Do not falter in your focus to create your paradise. You must hold on to that image. We need to accept the chaos and confusion and not fight it. We only need to concentrate our effort to replace it with our new vision and then a shift is inevitable.

This outdated system we have will surely erode and break down in order for our new vision to replace it. As I have said many times to you, you chose to be a part of this scenario, at this time, and on this planet. It is your wish to be here and an incredible time to be alive. Now you have to make a bigger choice. The choice of how you see your world going. It will be either the global dictatorship that is planned for you or a new free world, where we live in the paradise we have envisioned."

Falak stood motionless; she had never heard Alfonso in full flight. She had no idea how long it may go on for. Juan knew his capabilities and sat down on the edge of the bed.

"Remember also, you are never alone, meditation and prayer come free. Ask that mankind develops for the highest good of everyone on the planet and then trust the answer is coming in its own wonderful way. Express full appreciation that it has the wisdom to know how to deal with your request. Just allow the process to happen. Trust will ensure the outcome, doubt will destroy it. And, paradoxically again, you can do it alone, it is your experience and you can connect and disconnect whenever you desire. This is why I am the manager of my thoughts. I do not let a television set run my world; it stops you from thinking positively. It is a distraction, along with all the others on offer. Most people do not know how to think so they have it done for them."

He looked at Falak and Juan and nodded his head in approval of his own speech.

"How wonderful to see you both," he remarked, as if he had only just noticed them. "May I treat you to lunch? I know a lovely restaurant down the stairs. Afterwards we can walk to the threshing ground and sit on the rock of much wisdom. The last time Juan sat there he was the poor reeling receptacle of a madman's mutterings," he said to Falak, who donned a wonderful look of shell shock.

"It was quite a time for you wasn't it? I remember your young face Juan, so deep in thought, so naïve as I turned your world upside down. It wasn't easy for me either. You see Juan I have no children now, but I remember the innocence and trust there. I did everything in my power not to betray that trust in my son. Broke my heart to see his magic at my mercy and be the one responsible for negotiating the harsh realities of the truth of the world he had joined.

It's difficult work being a parent. You should both give great thought to this commitment. It is such a paradox, like everything in this universe; they are born with magic, absolute purity and full potential. They are between worlds and completely vulnerable, a blank canvas lay in a cot of corruption, unless the parents are free from shackles of normality. They believe in magic because there is magic. They see things we don't because they can look where we can't. And then we slowly convince them there is nothing to see until eventually they don't see either, because it's too difficult to continue with their truth. I tried to find a balance, encouraging his multi - faceted spirit while preparing him enough to survive the limitation of his peers. I think I did a good job too."

A vacant stare followed, a stare searching for something or someone too far to reach.

"I never knew you had a son Alfonso. I just assumed you had never been married. I don't know why. I can't believe I never even asked."

"It was many years ago now Juan," he said, putting his arm around him and comforting them both equally.

"Don't you miss them?"

"My understanding tells me that love can not disappear because it has temporarily left the limitations of our five senses. More than this, my sixth sense has allowed me the privilege of knowing the whereabouts of his re-incarnation."

"You mean you know where he is right now?" Juan said, a clear two semi tones higher.

"Sure do."

Juan thoughtfully juggled the balls of curiosity and tactfulness.

"If you don't mind my asking, how did it happen? I mean how did he die?"

They were both killed in a train accident in Italy. They were visiting my wife's family in Torino, she was Italian you see. I didn't go because I thought my work was more important. I used to be very industrious Juan, but when my wife and Carlo passed on I had to search for new truths to fit my new world. It would have been so much easier to have had the understanding and philosophy before I lost them both, than trying in a state of desperation to make sense of it all.

Anyway the more I opened up the more I was shown and the first time Carlo spoke to me and I heard him clearly, I realised there is but a thin veil separating us from the other side. Sometimes the thin veil feels like ten mile concrete block, it's true, but I realise that is only doubt possessing me in my weaker moments. You wouldn't think such a small head could carry ten miles of concrete would you?"

Juan was coming to terms with the fact that he had come to the mountains a second time and had fallen straight into the mystery school of Alfonso as he unfolded another chapter of his life.

"So you see I did not take the decision to put you on the path of truth lightly. I didn't know how often I would be seeing you. I knew for sure we were going to meet in these mountains, you know now about my ability to see into the future, it's no secret. So in those few hours I wanted to give you everything a parent normally has eighteen years or so to give. This is a beautiful ending to my story, to have this much contact with you Juan and to see the way you have turned out gives me more joy than you could imagine."

He walked up to Falak who had lost her look of shock and gained one of concern. He put his arm around her and guided her to the landing where she had stood less than ten minutes ago thinking Alfonso was dead in the bed, only to be completely shocked by his arrival as he lectured them on subjects out of this world, before breaking the news he had lost his wife and child in the past. A more unusual ten minutes she couldn't remember.

"Take the drinks downstairs you two; lunch will be ready in a few minutes. We will continue our conversation over a nutritious salad."

Alfonso was back within minutes. Falak was sitting at the same table she had used when she came with her family, momentarily lost in thought, attempting to make sense of the senseless. Juan was looking at his picture, transporting him back in time once more to the patio at Los Monteros, the magnanimous mountain, and the emotional minefield.

Alfonso picked up his conversation at the exact place where he had left it.

"I took a chance that day Juan, it was a risk to impart so much on one so young and I spent weeks in contemplation after you had left."

"You shouldn't have worried; I would not have had it any other way. Surely the measure of whether it was right or wrong to do so would have to be the level of my happiness now"

"It's a fair point Juan. My decision to open your mind so quickly was influenced firstly by the short time I had been handed, and secondly, I had faith in your ability to handle the information I was giving you by my memory of Carlo's personality. He was very receptive to the truth. I hoped you had carried some of that over into your present life."

Alfonso chewed on his food and waited for Juan to digest his words.

"How do you mean Alfonso, carried over?"

He put down his knife and fork and looked directly at Juan, knowing the next statement would carry the magnitude of the truth of the path most humans take. Not the ultimate truth I may add, but the truth for most.

"I have mentioned before that we go a long way back but you never asked me how or why."

"I just thought you meant everyone in general Alfonso, I didn't know you were implying... Well, what are you implying?"

"I am not implying Juan, I am informing. You used to live right here with me in these mountains. You were Carlo, my son."

It took Juan a few moments before his breath could be used for speech as well as survival. Falak's hand was searching for Juan's beneath the table in a futile attempt to outsmart freakishness with familiarity.

"You mean I used to be here with you?"

"That is what I just said."

"This is all very difficult to take in Alfonso."

"It is not such a strange phenomenon. It's only the fact that I have the ability to access other dimensions that gives it credence. It is happening right now to the whole planet, the same truth for almost everyone Juan, but for you the theory is now actualised."

"How can you be absolutely certain, I mean it can't be easy to know something as complex as this?"

"Don't you know it too Juan? When you open up and remove the blockage that tells you we are not family because different blood runs through our veins, you will know it too. Blood has nothing much to do with family. You know our connection is a strong one. Knowing, remember, is the absence of thinking. The universe is as simple as it is complex, as deep as it is shallow. We must always try to take as much rationale out of life as possible; it impedes our grip on reality. Our man made logic is the workings of an ignorant mind. I know from experience Juan, I have felt every emotion under the sun in my short lifetime, even times when ending my life seemed like the only option available to me."

He picked up his cutlery once more but returned them immediately to the table.

"Our emotions are an important part of life. I learned to accept them and work with them. Your mind however . . . , well, more of a hindrance than a help, unless tethered and trained. Now here I am, sat with you all these years later. It was the loss of you, my son, that sent me on a life long search, culminating in my ability to speak to those on other side and ending up with me being sat back here with you. If I would have known the outcome I may have relaxed into the ride more. But I have changed now, and you even more. We have evolved through our experiences together. This is how it all works. Death has only meant a change in your evolution. Look at us now; we are here in these mountains as we were before, two spirits in continual refinement."

"But how could you be communicating with me on the other side when I am born and living in this world?" Juan asked.

"There is even more depth to the situation than you may be aware of. Don't forget that we are multi-dimensional and time does not exist in other realms. Bi location is a distinct probability. We have much talking to do Juan and much time to do it in. We can waffle on for an eternity."

Juan turned to Falak and smiled at her. It felt like the only thing he could do.

"Well Falak, your universal father in law certainly took the surprise out of our surprise don't you think?"

Falak smiled at them both and reached over for Alfonso's hand, no words were needed, and a comfortable silence reigned on a strange key.

46

ENDINGS

In truth there is no beginning and no end. We have eternity woven into the fabric of our existence.

Florence and Jack were waiting in the pasture (a promise is a promise in any dimension) when Joseph arrived home. Roy had gone through to meet him to make the passing of the old and arrival of the new world easier, a loving and familiar face arriving right on time.

Joseph laughed as the realisation hit him that he had in fact only just left this comfort blanket of light which enveloped him once more, relieving him of all earthly ties. He thought about all he had been through, the emotions, the pain, the joy, years and years of drawn out drama, and he had only left home for a matter of moments. I must say he was momentarily overwhelmed at the peculiarity of it all.

Vivid and intense colours were all available to heal his spent spirit, re-energising and re-vitalising him.

And in a brown box, in a brown church lay the spent shell which had temporarily housed the indestructible spirit of Joseph. The people dressed in black sobbed through a service of mad morbidity, as a vicar with no real knowledge of Annabelle, and even less of the workings of the universe delivered his sub standard speech, which offered little in the way of a much needed explanation.

Some hymns of lyrical tragedy and musical misery were offered before a pair of curtains closed around the box to mark the end of this shockingly written saga called a funeral.

The box then disappeared to the furnace for the final twist of the knife of the macabre, as Annabelle's image resigned itself to family photo albums and failing memories. Joseph's spirit however soared in the cosmos and burned brighter than ever.

He was busy meeting his old friends and celebrating the return from his tiny trip out to Earth. Review and rest were the only items on the agenda, leaving the party to expand, drawing in more friends as the news about Joseph coming home spread.

Stories were told of one more rung on the universal ladder, successfully climbed.

Every story equals an experience; every experience is a success, good, bad or indifferent. Life can never be a failure. The ladder is always climbed and no life is ever wasted.

One by one the old friends returned home, boxes burned on earth and spontaneous celebrations in the universe welcomed each and every infinite spirit back home, the only tragedy being that the box burners knew nothing of the parties taking place. Invitations can not be issued to closed minds, and closing minds is the successful achievements of most church leaders, politicians, army leaders, pharmaceutical leaders, ignorant doctors, designers of the ill named education system, cheerleaders of corrupt sports, banking cartels, blind and ignorant scientists, deaf and dumb news readers, deluded journalists, and all the rest of the indoctrinated, from the traffic warden to the executioner, whether conscious or unconscious. It is time for you to wake up. The only power you have is in the uniform or the title someone has given you. You have no power yourself, the uniform, as an extension of the state and its corruption allows you to behave in the narcissistic way you do. When they have finished with you, when you have helped put into place the nightmare existence they provably have ready to install, they will discard you too. You and your children and grandchildren will be left trying to remember what a thought of your own was like. Sort it out before it's too late!

The last one to return home was of course Delmore. His lust for life and determination to break the spell cast on humanity thousands of years ago, had, along with his positive way of dealing with his health and wellbeing, enabled him to surpass one hundred Earth years. Feeling he had achieved all he could for one trip, he simply lay down in his home in the mountains of Las Alpujarras and waited to be escorted home.

Oh I forgot to mention that he had been living there for the last fifteen years, moving out of Morocco and the Costa del Sol after Falak had passed away. Having had no children of their own and with no other family left, he had spent his days painting, writing, and perfecting the techniques of Aikido and Ki exercises.

In an ironic turn of events he had filled the post of mountain mystic vacated by the passing of Alfonso. The sight of a sword swinging, agile old man doing finely honed mind and body co-ordinated movements, had for almost a century blessed this threshing field in Methina Fondales.

In his final hour on Earth, as he looked through his open window toward the mountain he had painted all that time ago, he saw the face of Alfonso appearing out of the vague waveform of energy lines, changing slowly into the perfectly formed and familiar face which now looked down at him from the corner of his room.

He smiled a welcoming smile as he offered his hand to Juan, lifting him gently through the window, shedding the heavy body of armour, spiralling out through the tunnel towards infinity and the great potentiality of a story without end and without limits.

Arriving at the peak of a blue and orange mountain he sat down with Alfonso, feeling all the Ki of the universe going into a point in his centre, and then instantaneously expanded outwards into infinity, one with the universe. He laughed at the naturalness of this universal connection and remembered how it had taken years of practice to achieve a similar feeling on Earth. He played with the concept of infinity for a while, allowing the absolute knowledge that he can never be destroyed wash through his body of light.

His thought's extended to his family and he immediately fell through the mountain with Alfonso in tow, floating down spirals of energy towards the pasture where he heard many voices simultaneously shouting his name.

He fell into the lightness of them all, his father and mother, sister and brothers, Hacham and Zahra, all he had encountered and seemingly lost along his path, and every time he remembered another friend they showed up instantly. Excitedly he remembered his promise to meet Joseph and Annie, Robert, Florence, Jack and his beloved Kitty at the pasture.

The luminescent vibrancy of light, a thousand times brighter than the world he had left behind massaged his spirit as he flopped down amongst the flowers, with the old gang appearing all around him. He saw Kitty, surrounded by children and instantly understood why as Falak, she had not been able to enjoy motherhood. She had been mother to thousands of young spirits for as long as he could remember and had agreed to pursue other things on her last visit. Delmore laughed at the heartbreak they had felt at not being able to conceive a child. "Reasons for everything," he said to himself, "reasons for everything."

"You took your time didn't you?" Joseph grinned. "We thought you were never coming home."

"Yes I think I got my money's worth. It's so incredible to be back home and all together."

"We knew you were ready. Falak was going to come and meet you but she had the idea of Alfonso coming, because of your location in the mountains. He had already visited you many times. You know he was very excited when you moved up there."

"I sure was," Alfonso replied. "Excited and surprised, I did not see that one coming. It's incredible that even when we know the exact outline of our incarnation, we still have a free hand in writing it as we go. We have the advantage of free will and of course so does everyone we interact with. We always affect each other with our choices and decisions in the physical state, but we still face the same difficulties and challenges with people we planned to meet before our birth. The important lessons are in the reaction to the action, the way we respond to these challenges. That is our free will.

You could have stayed in Morocco or the Costa del Sol, travelled the world or exited your incarnation through illness when you were finally alone. Do you remember now how you wrote in all those possibilities before you went? How you sat down with your guide and designed incident and accident for your growth?"

Delmore let the words of Alfonso and his friends wash over him, content to absorb their excited offerings, relieved at the disposal of his old tired body, and rejuvenated with his new feeling of lightness and brightness.

"I do remember, and I guess I will be doing it all again soon, but not yet. I've had a wonderful trip out, and loved almost every minute of it. Sometimes though, in those quiet moments or even in times of sheer bliss I found myself looking up towards the stars, aching for something I couldn't quite place. Homesick, that's what I was, it's what they all are Alfonso. Settled, yes, and even content, yet at the same time only ever a second away from feeling lost, isolated, and cut off. And we're so close too aren't we? I mean only a thought away from here."

"What about you Alfonso, any plans for your next visit?"

Alfonso smiled a smile of knowingness, love poured from his entirety and Juan collected the contentment.

"I will not be treading that path anymore Juan, things have happened to me while I was waiting for you to return, things are so much clearer now."

"In what way?" Juan asked.

"In every way Juan. I looked around at all this wonderment, all this we have created with our mind, and we are lucky Juan, we really are, lucky because we have created something fantastic."

"Isn't that a good thing Alfonso, I thought we had mastered things, you know, a bit of heaven, well it couldn't be better could it?"

"Yes and no Juan. We are ok I guess, but we are still not free, not really, I still feel attached to my mind, there is more to let go of. I mean we shouldn't have to keep repeating the cycle endlessly. We have created this between life bliss with our minds Juan, that's why there are so many different between life states, Christian heavens, Buddhist heavens, Islamic heavens, they are not one with consciousness, they are creating paradigms through their religious beliefs which still dominate their experience. We are still trapped in the mind Juan."

"Yes ok, let's say that it's true and we are still trapped in some kind of loop, what else is there? We have to keep going back to learn new things and also suffer the consequences of previous actions, surely we can't escape that."

"See Juan, you have just gone from describing it as heaven here to admitting we can't escape. Don't you feel it too? Yes, that's it, how can infinite consciousness or unconditional love, or that universal Godliness that just is, have anything to learn? It is all knowing isn't it? I may be a little off the mark but you know how we are manipulated on Earth and how knowledge is suppressed to protect the game plan, well it is even affecting us here in the after life. We are so much more than even this paradise here. Our soul is always resonating, when the body dies it is this resonance which decides where we go, what we experience next. They are deliberately keeping our soul from expanding down there, keeping us in the loop.

I had this conversation with you in those mountains remember, the reason I had no television, or didn't read newspapers or conform to the norms of the mainstream programme. But it is much bigger than that Juan. The manipulation is tremendous but it is coming to an end. I really believe that. When we collectively realise that we are spiritually handcuffed and we finally see our human form as just an experience from the perspective of being everything that is, we will vibrate at a higher resonance, high enough to break out of this reincarnation cycle. Right now we are victims of conditioning before we even arrive on Earth for more conditioning. I am determined to wipe out the lower vibrations of my soul that keep me repeating the endless cycle. We are all one Juan, we are all one."

Juan understood instantly. It had been his mantra on Earth and he was now being handed an opportunity to actualise the theory, one that was about to cut his last ties to a conditioned mind and an illusory existence.

"I was even thinking of being a guide for you in your next incarnation, I don't suppose . . ."

"No guide necessary," Alfonso interjected. "When you sharpen your intuition and perception, you will not need guiding. I will be flying solo for a while, conducting my own orchestra."

They held each other in one final moment of separateness, two columns of light merging into one, total understanding of what they had become. And what they had become was one.

So that's what happened more or less. My friends went on an excursion for some years by your reckoning, yet to me, were gone for a few moments. Much emotion and commotion took place, people were killing each other in silly uniforms which made them more of a physical man or woman but much less of a spiritual being. They will look back in clarity and cringe at what they failed to see as ridiculous at the time, but look back and learn they must, choosing bravely to return to Earth as perhaps a victim of extreme violence themselves, knowing that all rips in the fabric of spirit must be sewn with stitches of real understanding. Or perhaps not, if they become aware of their real self and reconnect with that real self to break free once and for all of the law of Karma, which is, like it or not, only one option or possibility and not a law set in stone.

They saw a planet of potential paradise being run as a prison and the prisoners virtually locking the doors on themselves, only having to say "no more" before walking out to the paradise already there. And remember the dark side is their own reflection too. If outer manifestation is the result of heart felt belief patterns, you are looking at the results of your world's collective thinking and feelings. No baddies and goodies, or them doing it to us mentality will save you now. Only a collective refusal to play the game of the global fascists will do it. And a love extended to each and every human on the planet will turn the whole world around. Give love to each other and everything will follow on from it.

Peaceful protest is good, refusing to pay taxes to corrupt governments is useful, but the wonderful trump card of refusing to join in anymore is enough for now, it's so, so powerful.

So earthlings, it's time for the action of non action, take your ball in and tell them you're not playing the game anymore. You can, and you must take back your planet, for the sake of your children, grandchildren, and all those others to come. And somewhere in the perceived future, if you so desire another trip, you will make it somewhere worth coming back to.

We are waking up
To the fact that we have been controlled for thousands of years
That you murder and lie and control us with fear
And you feed off that fear to hold your form
In your sinister side we're the ultimate thorn
We are waking up

To the "Common purpose" you cleverly speak
Through a slant on the Neuro linguistic technique
To the unsocial services stealing our kids
In courts with locked doors where you're taking the bids
We are waking up

To the military slugs that fly in our sky
Leaving their trail of poison behind
Attacking our immune system and crippling our minds
Aluminium and barium chem trailed skies
We are waking up

To the fact that you're fighting illegal wars
And weapons of destruction were not there at all
The dictionary labels that term "genocide"
And a murdered weapons inspector you label "suicide"
We are waking up

To the Satanist families running our planet
Those interbreeding bloodlines are beginning to panic
The veil has been lifted, revealing the men,
who are more scared of us than we are of them
We are waking up

To engineered viruses and death vaccinations
And the queen who controls uranium depletion
The Georgia stones and the de population
The 2012 fake alien invasion
We are waking up

Your Middle East takeover plans are well known
And towers can never collapse on their own
You misjudged us greatly and the truth movement grows
Your time's running out, soon the whole world will know
We are waking up

To the chemical cocktails in food and in drinks
Genetically modified, unable to think
Aspartame for children, a diet so poor
ADHD and the Ritalin cure
We are waking up

So prey to your serpents, and worship the moon
The fake, hollow sphere, we'll find you out soon
Your days they are numbered, you're losing control
We've got the power of six billion souls
And we are waking up

AFTERTHOUGHTS

I began writing the book in May 2008 on the island of Majorca. It was raining and we spent the afternoon waiting for the weather to improve. Fortunately I had taken my lap top with me, not that I ever used it much, I probably would have left it in its bag for the whole time we were in Majorca, had it not rained.

I had been thinking for a while of writing a short children's story dealing with the loss of loved ones, a simple explanation of re-incarnation which is not often explained to children. As I began typing that afternoon and the book began to take shape, it became evident something else was forming.

I kept the theme of re-incarnation but couldn't hold down the original idea of the children's book. It felt as though I had to rid myself of all my thoughts and beliefs, both gut instincts and studied theories, thrown in, often chaotic and with no apparent connection to the intended story. Even the story itself only really developed as I hit the keys, I didn't know where it was going or how to shape it, and having never written anything before I had difficulty in turning these feelings and thoughts into the structure necessary for a story book.

However, the more I wrote, the more information seemed to come my way, and often in bizarre ways. I say this not to make the story appear more mystical, but what strikes me is that as we apply ourselves intently to something, the focus and desire seems to allow a certain synchronicity and flow to develop. In my own case, as someone with no desire to be the author of a book of this nature, I was shocked at times as to the amount of words that seemed to flood out of me. This in itself was made more arduous by the fact I had never really typed before.

I make no apologies to the intellectually meticulous authors and book critics amongst you. I left school with virtually no qualifications and began working as an engineer at the age of just sixteen, and the rudiments of English grammar had remained unvisited since 1979.

I mention this not to excuse myself of any shortcomings in a literary sense but more to encourage expression and creativity without the need to show your profile of academia qualification. If it is judged to be a poorly written book so be it. If one person enjoys it and becomes enthused enough to shake off his/her shackles and have another look at where reality lies, then the effort has been worthwhile. Success for me is always in the creating and not in the results of the judges. I had a thought to write a book and I transformed doubt, procrastination, and general lethargy, into belief, focus, and sheer will power, until I saw my thought forms manifest at the end of a printer. What people make of it really doesn't concern me. That will be their story.

Grov Molovsky

THE CHARACTERS

The only definite connection to a real life person is the character Roy O Mally. Roy was certainly created from the essence of my father in law who passed over in March 2008. His passing was the initial reason I began to write the children's book. I wanted a way to explain to my five year old son where his granddad had gone.

The memory I had of this beautiful man had to be somehow positively captured. The character of Roy is as exact as I could have been, in the gentle way he spoke, in the kindness of his manner and in the sheer simplicity of his life. I am not sure why he never got to impart his wisdom on a grand scale but I don't think it was something he ever gave thought to. He was just happy to live his life moment by moment. It was such a pleasure and honour to be able to convey my feeling for him in the pages he occupied, as it was to share the little bit of time we had together this time around. I hope the readers will be inspired by his character. He is a worthy inspiration.

AIKIDO

I have been studying the martial art of Aikido for the last twenty years. Some of the theories and techniques in the book have certainly been influenced by the many hours I have spent in the do-jo. I have had the great fortune of having Sensei Kolesnikov 7th dan instructor as my teacher and friend. He has been teaching professionally for over thirty five years and ranks, in my opinion, amongst the best instructors in the world. If you are interested in his teachings you will find his contact information under useful resources.

USEFUL RESOURCES

www.wearewakingup.org

Campaign for truth in medicine – Dr Philip Day
For information on disease prevention, diet and all health needs.
www.credence.org

To uncover the truth on all global issues.
www.davidicke.com

To fully understand how the term "common purpose" affects us all.
Also for advice on returning the right of the British people to govern
themselves.
www.briangerrish.com and www.lawfulrebelion.org

Another good source of information on exposing the New World
Order is Jim Corr from the band The Corrs. You can find him at
www.jimcorr.com

Another great website is www.tpuc.org

For information on Wasyl Kolesnikov 7th dan international Aikido
teacher, whose photographs feature in the book.
www.universalaikido.com

For instructional DVD's on mind and body co-ordination, infinite tai
chi, meditations, breathing exercises, philosophy etc, visit
www.harmony-with-the-universe.co.uk

To join an active group regarding chem trails visit chem trails UK on
facebook.com